A NEW WORLD

THE ARCADIAN CHRONICLES

M. L. Rusenik

A NEW WORLD
THE ARCADIAN CHRONICLES

M. L. Ruscsak

The Arcadian Chronicles

Trient Press
3375 S Rainbow Blvd
#81710, SMB 13135
Las Vegas,NV 89180

Ordering Information:
Quantity sales. Special discounts are available on quantity purchases by corporations, associations, and others. For details, contact the publisher at the address above. Orders by U.S. trade bookstores and wholesalers. Please contact Trient Press: Tel: (775) 996-3844;   or visit www.trientpress.com.

Printed in the United States of America

Publisher's Cataloging-in-Publication data
Ruscsak, M.L.
A title of a book : A New World: The Arcadian Chronicles
ISBN Hardcover
      Paperback
      E-book

A New World

Dedication:

For my dad who is missed every day. And for light in the darkness who lights the path from the darkness.

A New World

Dear Readers,

Thank you so much for joining me on this journey. Though this is the final book in the Lite and Darke series is on the horizon the tale does not end there.

For with every story there is more than one point of view. And in order to know the truth you must know all the knowledge. To understand everything please be on the look out for The Obsidian Chronicles and the Chronicles of Cronan. But to keep moving forward Legends of the Mind will begin oh so soon.

But please remember with everything I write everything is intertwined. And just because you read it does not mean it is truth. Just because you see it , it may only be half of the story.

Dig deeper because this story is about to be torn apart and the pieces may not fit back together.

Happy Reading

M. L. Ruscsak

A New World

The Arcadian Chronicles

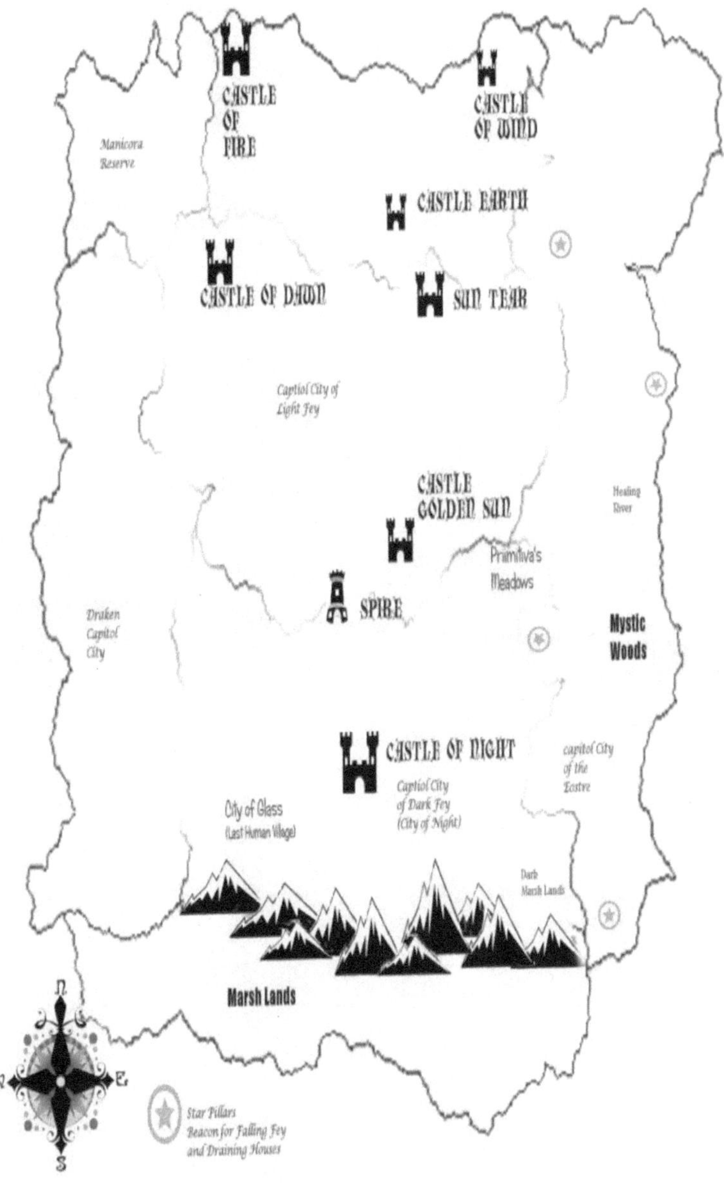

A New World

Athenaeum
Lumaista
Akrsna
Anahita
Osirus
Alaunus
Fauna
Pallas
Aurora
Lucerne
Flyta
Ignatius
Erembour
Lite and Darke
Tomb of the unknown
Obsidian

A New World

Pallas
Aurora
Flyta
Nexus
Tomb of the Unknown
Obsidian
Calacatta
Silica
Athenaeum
Floraian
Nimbus

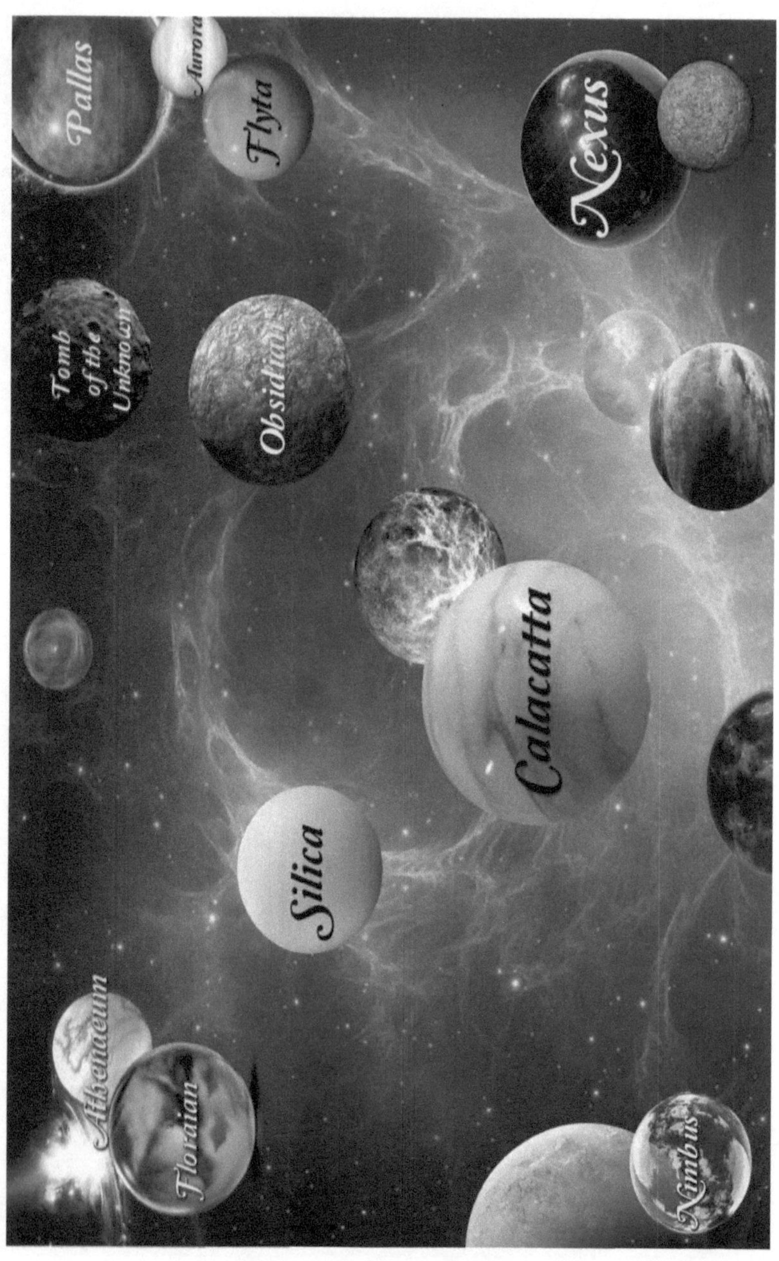

The Arcadian Chronicles

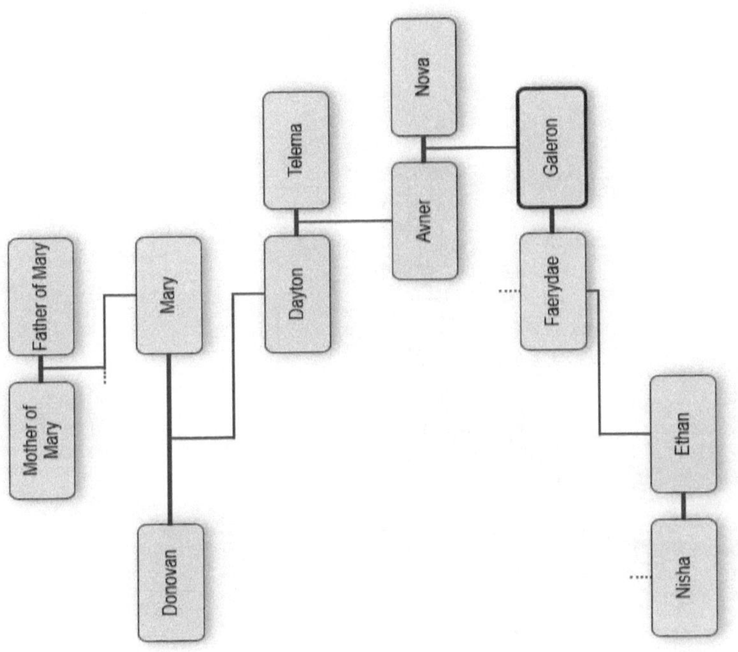

A New World

David
Glyndwr
Celesta
Lilly Kairavi
Ciardha Aidan
Vasilllissa Trovos
Blake Kairavi
Azia
Griffith
Orenda
Myrddin Devros
Pythia
Father of Enya
Enya Queen of Life
Mother of Enya

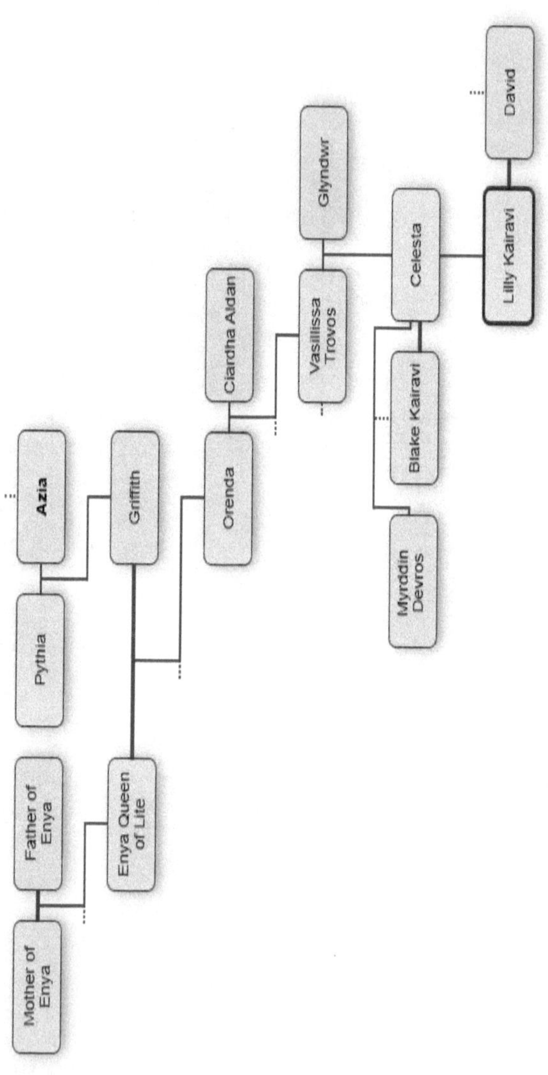

The Arcadian Chronicles

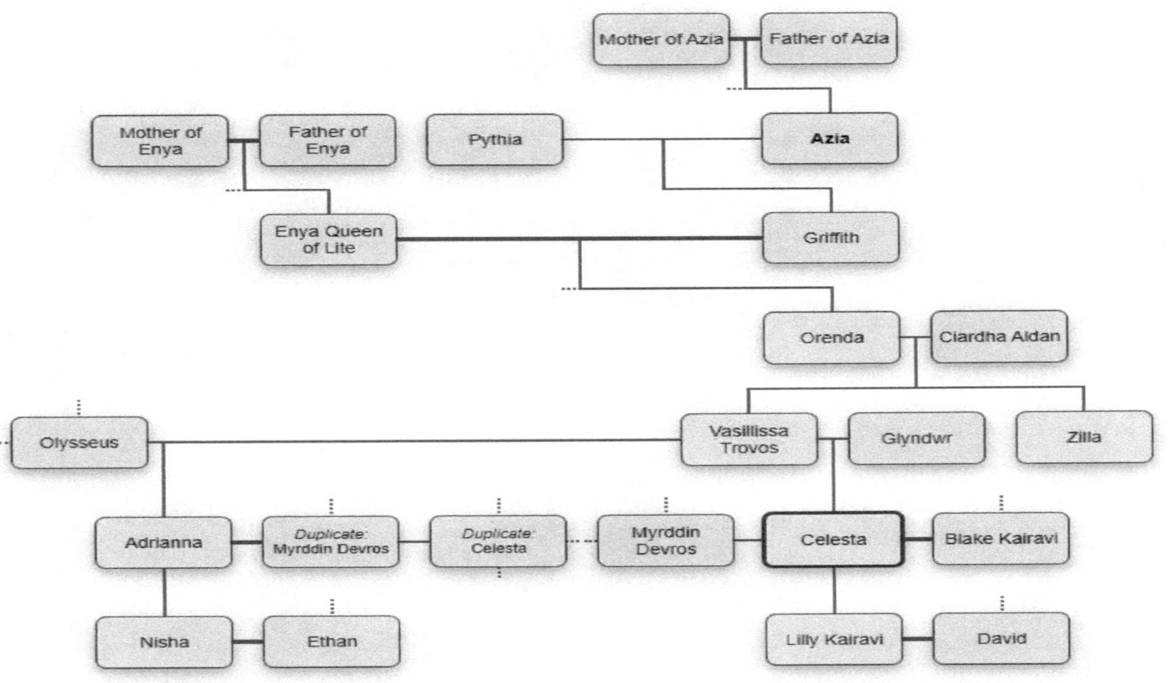

A New World

Mother of Azia
Father of Azia
Pythia
Azia
Enya Queen of Lite
Griffith
Aldan
Orenda
Ciardha Aldan
Glyndwr
Olysseus
Vasillissa Trovos
Zilla
Anon 30
Celesta
Blake Kairavi
Adrianna
Myrddin Devros
Lilly Kairavi
David
Nisha
Ethan

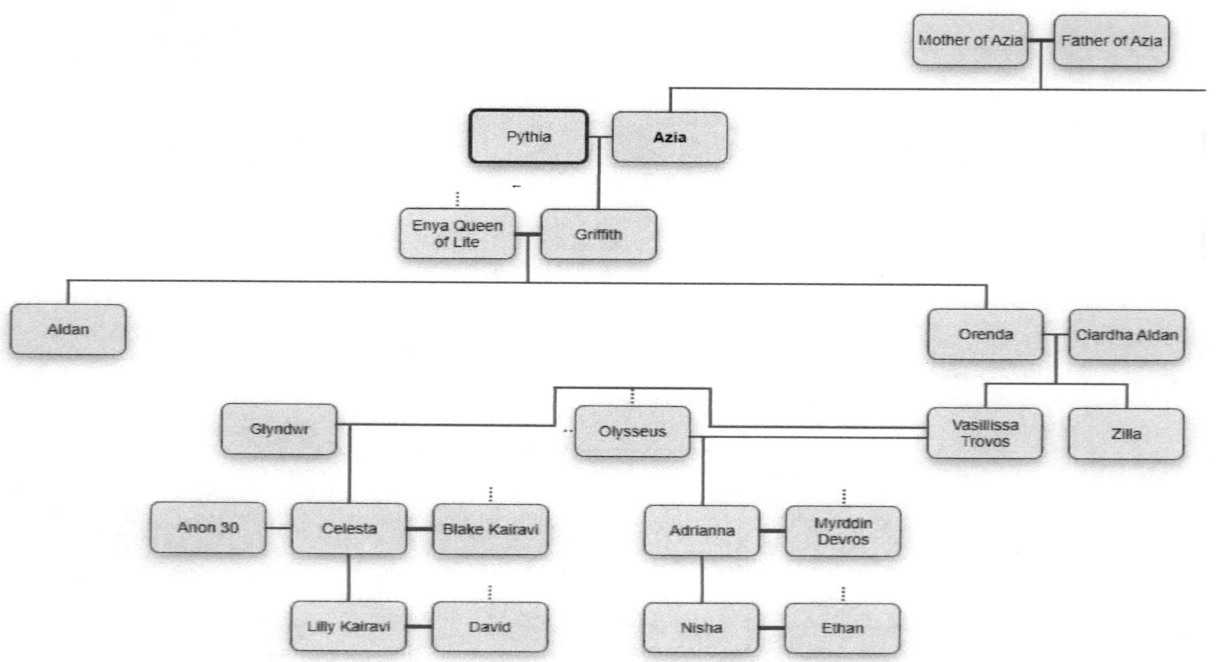

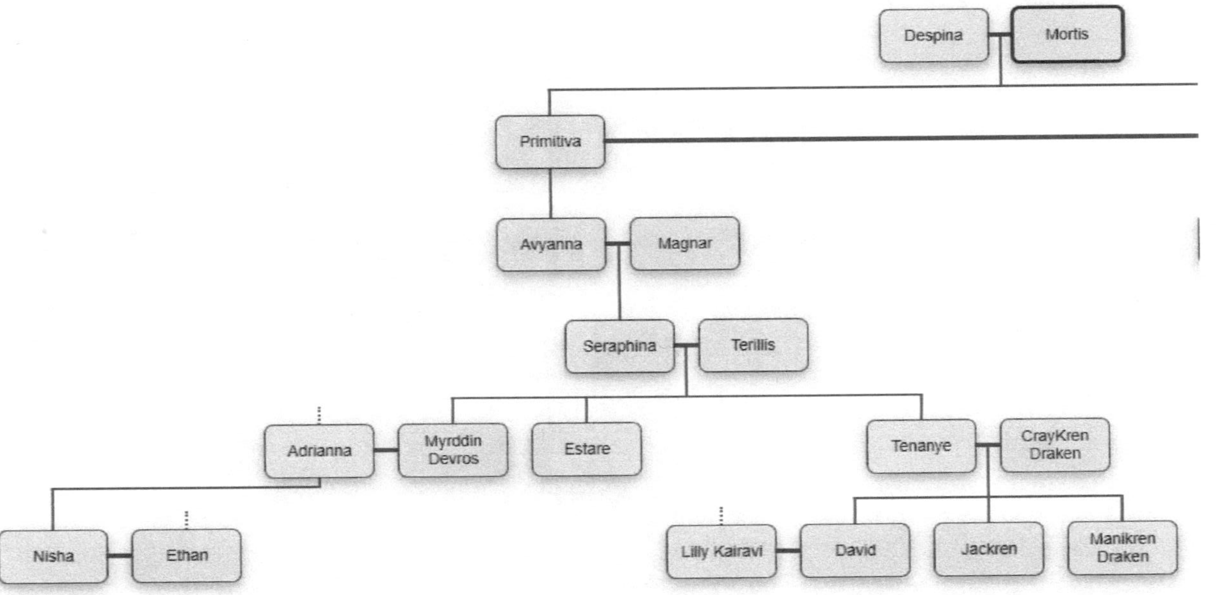

Despina
Mortis
Primitiva
Avyanna
Magnar
Seraphina
Terillis
Adrianna
Myrddin Devros
Estare
Tenanye
CrayKren Draken
Nisha
Ethan
Lilly Kairavi
David
Jackren
Manikren Draken

A New World

Alex
Ari
Mortis
Despina
Magnar
Primitiva
Avyanna
Terillis
Seraphina
Estare
Celesta
Myrddin Devros
Adrianna
Ethan
Nisha
Tenanye
Cray'Kren Draken
Manikren Draken
Jackkren
David
Lilly Kairavi

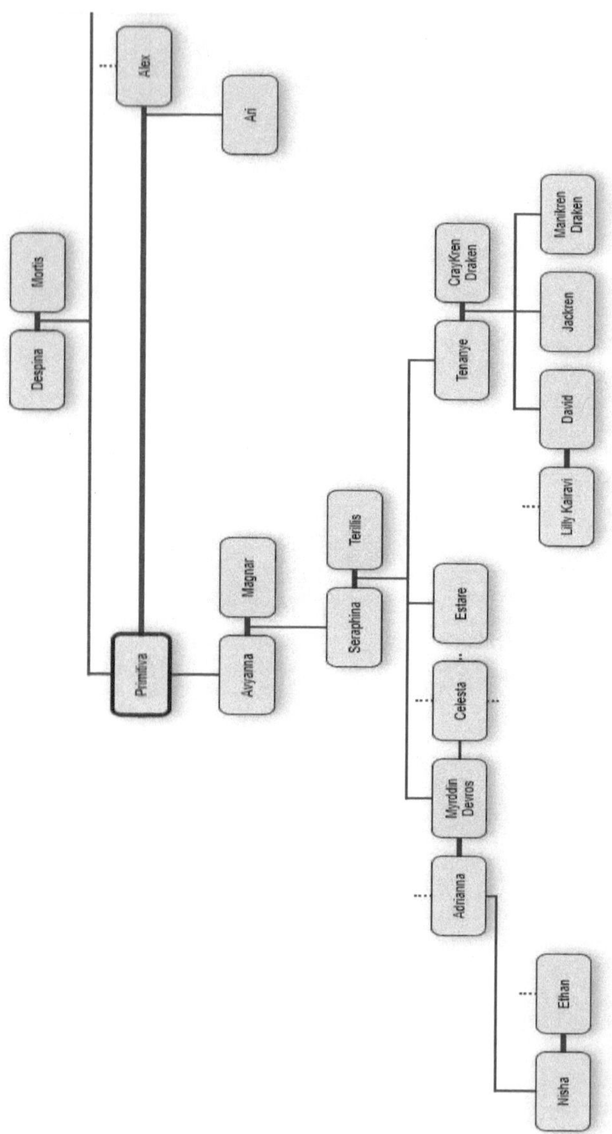

The Arcadian Chronicles

A New World

PROLOGUE: AKRSNA

Aanshi pulled back from her looking glass. Not many knew she was a seer and for those who did, ah well their tongues as their loyalty belong to her. Taking a claiming breath she steadied herself. Slowly she covered the looking glass with the dark cloth. More for show than for need to keep things hidden.

Only a seer could use it. And only she could gain entry withing this room.

A few deep breath before turning to her most trusted guards. Small adjustments to her green dress that suited well against her bronze skin. Her hair draped around her long enough to be a shawl. Yet it was the crown upon her head that gave her the power that was needed.

"Have my consort brought to me. The rest of you I'll speak to you shortly."

She didn't dismiss them. Didn't give then answer to any question. But they would remain in her private room guarding her looking glass.

Not that anything could destroy it, or get near it, but they would guard it just the same. All of them facing the single entry point to this room… the heavy wooden door that she alone could open.

A New World

She entered her bed chamber watching the black candles flicker in their holders. The crushed red velvet soft under her feet. Soon her consort would arrive and they would reach an agreement of what needed to be done. Words spoken now would decide the war that was still many light cycles away. Yet it would her , the Queen of Akrsna that would decide the fate of all the fey.

"My queen?"

Proper words coming from his soft tenor voice. He would behave as her consort while eyes were upon him. In truth he was her most trusted confidant. The man she allowed to rule over the armies. He was as ruthless has he was hansom. The brother or Azia. Thou if any knew that… ah, well it didn't matter.

A beat of silence the door clicked shut and the lock in place. None would hear them, nor would they dare.

"Our daughter as done well by her boy. He grows stronger by the day. However we have decision to make."

Mabuz carefully walked over to the bed. It was the only suitable place for him to be seated other then her dainty chair where she would brush her hair. No the bed was the best choice of seats even if he would rather stand. "What have you seen?"

She was fay looking in on children that were sent as consorts to other cities was beneath her. Yet she was still a mother, and her child would always be her child.

Of course that couldn't matter. Not today.

"Akrsna will decide the outcome of the great war. Arae will choose the side we deem for her. Both will be the beginning of the end for all fey."

"That tells me nothing." he paused shifting his weight just enough to show it was the queen's general asking and not her consort, "What is my brother's hand in this? And who stand against him?"

Aanshi shook her head. "This is long after his rule. Another more reckless will ascend. His child and your bothers stand against him. Our grandchild stands with them. Yet each side searched for the …"

"For Arae. They seek something that can't be control without a price."

"Is that what you think? That I do not control Arae…"

Green mist started to cover the floor the black candles no longer dripping wax but blood. The smell of death hung in the air. "I control Arae as my blood before me has done. Yet it is your blood that will decide who will rule long after my bones turn to ash."

His eyes locked on hers never wavering. Anyone else would cower from the rage with in her. Anyone else would have been dead when the poison mist filled the room. He was not anyone else. "No, it is your blood that will decide. Nor mine. I have never wanted to rule and none without the blood of the first would ever survive Arae's wrath. I just pray his temperament is that of his father's and not that of our daughter's."

A sly smile filled her narrow face, "So you do know what your youngest is up to?"

"Some one had to keep the army sharp should she decide to take on Pallas."

3000 years before the Great war

"The stars have aligned and it breaths new hope for all of the star cities. A whisper of fear still echos through our lands. But hope can chase the darkness away…

Unless the whispers know what we do not."

-unknown

From the lost scroll of Akrsna

A New World

CHAPTER 1: ARCADIAN

The fire blazed in the forge. The fire giving his room a haunting glow as head and dust swirled around. His hammer hit the glowing red metal in front of him. Metal clanged. Sweat dripped from his short hazelnut hair. Wiring fell from his work bench. No matter it wasn't needed yet. First he needed this sheath then he would figure out how to attach the wires.

A soft cough from behind him. No need to look behind him. None. Not when he was the crown prince of Arcadian and he was in his private work room.His private sanctuary.

Pausing for only a moment he spoke letting his intrude know that he was aware of him, "I had an idea on how to enhance the shields and outer defenses."

A deep sigh, but his father would never openly criticize him. After all, it was he who had taught him the art of the forge and helped hone some of the most delicate designs.

A heavy withered hand resting hand on his shoulder as his father peered around to look at the metal circle. "What gauge wiring are you thinking?"

A New World

A common teacher to apprentice question when said in that tone. Good he had the old man intrigued. "I'm thinking 30 gauge." He paused dunking the red hot metal into the bucket of cold water. "What do you think about trying the fiber optic cable."

"Hmmm, it's still new and we haven't tried it outside of the communication hubs." His father pulled back wandering around the room of haphazardly laid tools and shavings of metal. His muscles ripping under the his armor. "How soon do you think you can have it running?"

Not an idle question. He wasn't speaking to his father or even his mentor. He was being asked a question by the King of Arcadian.

The tone didn't sound right. But he couldn't ask. Not yet.

Squaring his shoulders he took a deep breath. "If I have the guild's help I think we can do a test as soon as tomorrow."

A quick turn and something flickered his his father's eyes. "Get it done. I want the battlements prepared as soon as possible." Then his father gave a smile that always meant trouble, "And Govard, you are the crown prince not some ordinary Fey. You should be proud of your wings."

In his two hundred light cycles he had never felt the need to allow his dark blue wings be shown. Never felt the need for the woman of Arcadian faun over how the red and white veins ran over the flesh as delicate as wiring covering the latace outside of the throne room.

Yet this was his father's attempt at trying to get his son out of the workroom and doing something else… like finding a suitable bride.

"They get in the way while I'm working."

Two steps and father was standing before him. His brown hair starting to gray at he sides. His hands no longer that of a young man but one in the later years of his prime. "You are my son and I will always support your work. But you are also the crown prince, you need a bride."

"I know. But the women here…" he turned picking up some wiring just to have something to do with his hands. "… they are dull. I've known all of them since I was a small child and I can't think of any that I can see spending my life with. None that I see standing on the battlements should a conflict start."

Lines of laughter filled his father's face even if he never let the sound slip his lips. "My boy, I never said anything about finding a bride here. Go visit the other star cities, or find a seer to point you int he right direction."

"A… seer? But…"

Drawing closer he leaned in as close to Govard's ear, "They dwell on the dark stars." Stepping back he placed his finger to his lips, "Speak not of that. But give Abdou my regards."

The streets were lined with lighting. Orbs of colors on poles of polished steel. Cobbled streets made from the finest stone from any of the star cities.

This was his father's legacy. Trade routes. Finding ways to give the people light on the darkest of nights. The Guilds where contraptions were discussed and made into prototype had been his grandfather's legacy.

But what would be his legacy? What would he leave behind for the next generation of fey?

Legacy's were built on passion and desire. Built hand in hand with the help of the queen. Built for the betterment of their people and one day the betterment of all fey.

Govard looked around the streets. His skin glistening from sweat and speckled with dirt. The unattached woman watching him. Too many trying to attract him by puffing out their breast. Turning just enough to give their form more curves. Not one of them appealed to him.

How could anyone be attracted to woman who try that hard to win a warrior's heart. No maybe he would seek out a seer. Or at the very least get away from here for a short time.

Yes… yes he would do that just as soon as this idea was made possible.

His foot posed at the first step of the guild. The all building housed so many. Outside of the castle it was largest building in the whole of the city. But it wasn't the building that caught his attention. A streak of white light darting across the void. A messenger going from one city to another.

Shaking his head he opened the double doors. "When will the other cities understand our communication hubs can relay a message without ever leaving the city?"

It wasn't said to anyone directly yet all movement withing the large room ceased. Fey clothed just enough to save them from injury from burns but not so much not to see their muscles and true forms. All of them, nearly two hundred men, watched him.

A loud clap from the back of the great hall and the men started going to and from. Weaving in and out of the work benches. While an older fey approached him.

"Abdou?"

A New World

He crossed his arms shaking his head. His silver hair long past the days of his prime. "You are your mother's son. She is the only one since this guild was created that could get every worker to stop what they are doing."

"Yes well, mom does demand attention."

Abdou rolled his eyes. He wouldn't agree but he also would never disagree the truth of that statement. "Come tell me what you are needing and how soon do you need it done?"

A little chuckle slipped past his lips, " I have a design to increase the shields and fortify the battlements… if it works." he paused blowing out a breath, "Father wants a prototype by tomorrow."

A low whistle, "Must have something to do with the on goings of Obsidian and Lunaista. Or the rumors coming from Pallas."

The rumors of Pallas weren't just rumors. Not that he could say that. Arcadian had spies on most of the star cities. From those who held positions as guards to a few that were consorts to either the king or queen. But only a few knew that. And none outside the war room would discuss it.

"I'm sure my father only wished to build to his legacy to be more than just some pretty lights and cobbled stone."

Abdou paused and slowly looked Govard up and down. Slowly he leaned in. "Your father's legacy is you, never forget that." Pulling back he took his normal stoic stance, "Now what of this design?

A bit of mischief lit Govard's eyes. "I was thinking of playing with the fiber optics an tapping into the power of Arcadian."

"Ah, so trying to blow something up. Well at least you are giving me fair warning."

A New World

CHAPTER 4: PALLAS

The morning light stuck the place allowing light to shine over the great city. Streets of gold gave way to homes with lavish gardens. Beauty all round. And why shouldn't this grand city be the most lavish of them all? It was in fact the capitol of all of the star cities.

The center of the realm. The light of the void. The home of all of the secrets that only he the great Azia would ever know.

Stepping out onto his balcony Azia pulled his robes around him. Maybe a show of modesty but more so his citizens didn't take notice of the loss of some his muscles.

Stepping over to the low rail he allowed himself this time to take in all that Pallas had to offer.   The lush, mystic gardens. Vibrant green with flowers of a rainbow of colors. But those gardens had a secret.

Ah yes. A dark and terrible one that only a few knew and even they wouldn't speak of. At least if they wanted to live.

A small smile formed upon his face as he took a sip of his wine. While he watched he could feel the gardens draining the life, the power from every fey that tended them. He could see the outlines of those fools basking in the heat to keep the flowers pristine.

Turning his hand over he called in his looking glass wishing to see the gardens more closely. One of the workers fell to his knees. His body little more than skin and bones. It didn't take long for the guards to collect the man.

Perhaps they would feed him and allow him to rest. Perhaps he would be set to the prison to live out the reminder of his days. Either way he wouldn't live to see another full light cycle.

Taking another sip he let his mind settle in on a recent rumor. Not long ago one the queens gave birth the most dreadful of creatures. A child with dragon wings. The power that the star was now feeling was intoxicating , yet the fear of the demon child growing with every passing day.

Yes even here in the palace of Pallas he was tasting the power in the winds. One day he would feast upon that power. Draining what he wished and feeding the rest to his most honored citizens.

He laughed to himself. They would think it a great feast to be able to dine upon a creature such as powerful of that one. In truth they would be given just the scraps. Nothing more.

But not yet. No, the child must be allowed to grow until the first born is ready to rule. Not much longer now just a few more light cycles. Then , ah yes then he would have his prize.

Entering his thrown room he bellowed " Guards!!"

Armor clanked as two men rushed into the room. Azia's back turned toward them. A beat of fear from both men. It had been long known that those that served the thrown directly were often killed. Their bodies mutilated for entertainment. What was left dragged to the gardens and often buried there even before they had taken their last breaths.

Not serving the post. Well that was a fate worse then death.

Taking a steady breath the guard asked, "What are your orders , your majesty?"

Azia barely glanced over his shoulder, " See that my young bride has the encouragement she needs to not hinder the baby that is growing inside her." He paused just long enough to turn and scowl at the the men. "Then bring me a messenger."

The guards tip there head in respect as they said, "Yes sir!" then hurried from the room. Before the the double doors closed both paused seemingly not caring about the orders they had just received.

He had the mind to haul both of them back in here. To strip them of their flesh. BAH!

That would do nothing to remedy the problem. Nothing.

Pacing the length of the room he muttered to himself, " The citizens and rulers of the Star Cities are getting too comfortable. It's about time that I remind them that

All of the power resides in Pallas. I have taken notice of how they've grown complacent, lazy, and sloppy in their actions. Instead of living their lives with purpose, intent, as I've instructed, their lives must be lived for their own enjoyment."

His voice got louder as he yelled to the empty room, " I am the King of Kings! It is only by my terror and will that they exist. They shall remember that it is ME! Not their Goddess who wills them to live. I am God, Ruler, and the ONLY Divine power that matters. That it is I who chooses their fate."

CHAPTER 3: ARCADIAN

A loud whoosh just heartbeat before BANG. The explosion rocking the room but thankfully the building didn't have signs of collapse. Coughing Govard made his way thru the smoke filled room and opened the large thick double doors before falling to his knees.

His eyes still filled with blinding water which kept him from   seeing the two men rushing over to help him. Each gripping an arm and leading him away from the room. A few minutes longer and they would have everything back to rights. Well everything in the room anyway.

A heavy hand patted his back. He didn't need to see to know who would be watching him instead of cleaning up the mess. Coughing once more he wheezed out, "Need to adjust the power flow. Maybe add a converter."

"I see, so you are still convinced the power that comes from the star it's self can be harness into energy?"

Shit. Not Abdou. Nor was that voice the sound of his father. "Grand-père?"

The older fay glared at him. Some thought he had died several light cycles ago. Others whispered he retired to Pallas to live out his days in the golden pools. But those who lived in the guild knew the truth. The once King of

A New World

Arcadian dwelled here teaching what he knew to all those who would listen.

Oh he stayed mostly hidden in the lower battlements, but every once and awhile he would venture to the main hall.

With the smoke finally clearing his eyes Govard looked up at the man who had yet said a sound. "It can be done."

"Bah! You think I don't know that it can be done? Of course it can, you twit. But you can't just jam cables into a living thing and expect it not to react." He paced back and forth muttering dark curses. Venting a little bit of his anger.

Govard watched silently. No use trying to explain until his grandfather was calmer. So he would watch the man pace, his leather apron covering his front while his smoke gray wings rustled with agitation.

A few breaths more, "Can you explain what living thing you were referring to?"

Lakas stopped and turned suddenly. Before Govard could react , his wrinkled hand connected with the back of the youth's head. "The star you twit. The star is a living thing. How would like to be jabbed with cabling."

Old? Senile? Both were a possibility, yet the man had ruled over this star for more than a thousand light cycles. Lived at least twice that. So there could be an wisp of truth in that. "Ok, fine. The star is a living thing. So how does one connect cables to it?"

"How does… How… you.."

"Father?"

At the voice Lakas turned, "Your boy has his mother's brains. And none of her listing skills."

"Ah, but he has his Grand-père's curiosity. And his mother's skill with a blade. Now, who would like to explain why the testing lab blew up?"

He ha came here as the head of the family, but it was the king who had asked the question. Taking a deep breath Govard gave a half smile, "I made the first prototype and was testing it. The shield held for a breath before the energy became unstable resulting in the explosion."

He paused letting both of the men take in what he had just said. When both were glaring at him once again he smiled, "It's an good way to destroy the battlement."

Shaking his head Lakas growled, 'Why would we destroy the battlement it would…."

"To prevent our enemies from using our weapons against us."

Her voice was that of a autumn breeze. Her dress of leaves in motion. She look frail, but that as just because her true self was always cloaked. Always hidden so only those who she trusted knew she was fit today as the first day she arrived on this star. And her powers were just as strong.

Standing, he made his way over to he and kissed her cheek, "Mother?"

She patted his cheek and smiled, "You will be the death of me yet. But you mean well.' Locking her eyes with Daedalus, "it will be needed but not now."

For a moment both kings stood still then Lakas patted Daedalus on the back. "She's your wife so trust her. And keep the boy from destroying the whole damn star."

He didn't stay and listen to whatever had brought his mother from the castle. If she said the battlements would need to be destroyed his father wouldn't hesitate. But it begged to question why she had been the one to say it?

Just another oddity as of late. Growing into his full powers were going to be disturbing. At least according to both of his parents.

No matter he would have time to ponder that after he decided what star city to visit. Maybe Nexus. It was THE dark star to visit if one wanted to be scared shitless for a good lite cycle. But there were no finer dark fey out there. Or at least that was what the rumors said.

"Still pondering how to blow things up?"

Ah hell his father sounded amused. And amused was never good . "Actually I was thinking of visiting Nexus."

A deep sign,"You are your mother's son I swear more the you are mine. But first things first."

Oh bloody hell. "Am I talking to my father or the king?"

Daedalus gave him a sideways glance, "Both."

Oh sweet darkness. Either he was going to get his ass kicked by his mother or be on the receiving side of one his grandfather's lectures. "Wonderful, so who did I managed to piss off the most?"

His father he could say that to, the king… ah, well…

"Your mother wants whatever you did taught to those who man the battlements. The day will come when we see war. No matter what we cannot allow our technology to fall in the hands of the enemy."

That made sense. A lot more than he was ready to say. "Fine, If I use the testing room I can recreate the um… er … accident as many times as needed. Will the king be willing to explain this to the forge master?"

The look on his father's face was priceless. Laugh lines and the way he he was pressing his lips together was almost enough for him to laugh as well. Yet some how he managed not to.

"Yes, I think the king would be willing to remind the forge master of who rules this star." His father paused , "Now, before you leave for Nexus there are things your grandfather and I need to discuss with you."

"Is this about choosing a bride? Because I'm sure I do not need that kind of help."

"No, there are things the crown prince needs to know. And the knowledge will be a heavy burden."

Never had his father ever sounded so somber. Not when taking about something he, the crown prince, had to learn. So whatever this was, it was something he would never forget.

He walked beside his father for what seemed like forever. Deep within the castle. Well under the deepest of rooms. And yet the tunnel was well lit and cared for.

"Where are we?'

"Everyone thinks the cobbled streets and decorative lights are my legacy. What I would leave behind for the next generations. It isn't." Daedalus stopped taking a long deep breath, "When I married your mother she required a dark space. In truth she still does. Light brings out her temper in a way few will ever see."

"Which explains why the lights of the city and those here in the castle are an array of colors but not bright as those on Pallas."

"That is exactly why." Daedalus agreed before staking another step. "But there is more to your mother. The Queen of Akrsna is her mother, to this you know. But her father is the great general of Pallas. When Azia ascended the throne the general vanished."

"The story says Azia as his fist act as king declared all royal children not the first born to be killed or sold to other cities. From what is said, he ran this blade threw the general then buried him in the garden before he drew his last breath."

"Mabuz did have the blade of the king pierce him. And he was to be buried in the kings garden. That much is true. But, the kings and queens of the other star cities were there to witness the crowning. What happen then is a bit of mystery, however he ended up married to Aanshi."

It took several breaths before Govard dared to speak. Dared to put words to the thoughts he was now having. His bloodlines now traced to three of the star cities. Traced back to the Azia and Pallas. "So what does that mean exactly."

"It means, my boy Akrsna will always be your ally and Pallas will forever wish to destroy you."

Just like that. His father didn't mix words. He had always been direct with his response. And always, always clear when giving information.

Shaking the thoughts off Govard shook himself, "So what is this place?"

Turning slowly Daedalus smiled, "The Labyrinth."

Looking at his father and being given a nod to move forward Govard pushed open a large stone door. Then sucked in a breath as dim lights started to flicker on. Tunnels, weaponry, in the horizon what looked like a city.

Placing his hands on Govard's shoulder, "This is the city your mother saw in a vision. When Arcadian falls this will be were our people will be safe."

"Father?"

"War is coming, but we do not see the face of the enemy. The battlements will fall and with your help it will look like the enemy laid waste to the city."

He understood now. "Retreat to safe ground. Some will die in battle. But those who survive…"

"Will rebuild and fight when they are truly needed."

A New World

CHAPTER 4: PRIMITIVA

Frustrated beyond all reasoning, she picked up her crystal brush and plopped down at her vanity. As her brush passed through her fiery red hair she counted. "One. Two." Gritting her teeth, she pulled the brush through her hair as she slowly hissed, "Three." Taking a deep breath, she opened her dark soulless eyes. Her parents were talking about her… again. Debating if they should make her a tribute to the city of stars or marry her off to one of the other royal star families. Slamming her crystal hairbrush down on her vanity, she shattered both. Upset and pissed off she pushed away from her now destroyed vanity no longer caring if her hair was perfectly smooth or a fiery mess. No longer cared enough to shed the tears that she had so many times before

She no longer cared about much of anything.

Holding back the tears, she held in all of her strong emotions.

Her hurt. "If you're going to kill your children why ever have more than one?" She growled to herself. Her parents were not only not in the room, but were deep within the depth of the palace. But not deep enough where she could not hear them when she so chose. See them whenever she pleased. There was nowhere in all the Star Cities that she couldn't reach… couldn't see.

A New World

Not that any ever believed her. Not that any dared to.

Another breath, then she turned to her door. Not much of a door when you could see through it… you could see through everything except a single room in the palace. And that room was off limits to everyone except the queen herself. Frustrated, she turned away from her door. Nothing was private on this miserable star. Nothing.

"Don't even think about knocking, dear sister." She snapped, letting her thundering voice rattle the shards of crystal that now lay on her floor.

As the glass door opened, her sister smiled even though her sister turned from her, "Primitiva? You are more agitated than usual. Why?"

Damn her sister. The Crown Princess Starlis. Glaring at her sister, she dared not say what was on her lips. Instead took in her sister's rare beauty. Golden rays tumbled down her back, shimmering in the light of the room. Silver speckles dancing on her skin. But it was her eyes, the eyes of the galaxy that saw everything. "I will not marry a man who wishes only to have my power for his own."

"Ah. So, our parents are at it again? Trying to keep you from the tribute and yet you refuse."

As she turned her fire red hair wrapped around her revealing her wings. Wings that she was warned several times to never let be seen. "The only reason I am still here is because of Avyanna."

Starlis rushed over to her nearly placing her hand over Primitiva's mouth. Whispering, she said, "Shhhh. You know better than to speak her name."

Pushing her sister away and nearly allowing her to tumble, Primitiva hissed, "She is my daughter and I will speak her name whenever it pleases me."

Regaining her balance and closing the distance between them Starlis whispered, "You will get her killed. Now hush. I cannot protect her if you do not protect yourself."

Her sister was right, but only partly so. "You're right. I cannot protect her while I am still in Lunaista." Then she turned sharply.

She needed only, but a moment to decide what to do next. Only a moment to figure out how to bring about the change that the Star Cities needed.

A sigh of relief, then, "Finally, you are seeing reason."

Another moment to decide, "Which is why I am leaving."

Closing her eyes Starlis tried again to reason with her impulsive younger sister yet again, "You cannot just leave. There is nowhere in the Star Cities that you could go and not be found. Not that you could get to any other Star City." She let her eyes slowly open as she took a deep breath and tried to remind her sister, "Only messengers can go between the Star Cities and they have special training and abilities to do so."

As the second child, her powers… her abilities had been left untrained… even so, there was no one more powerful… no one… not even her dear sister. And certainly not that fool Azia who ruled Pallas. Slowly the room filled in a black mist. Not uncommon since she did this whenever she wished for privacy. Not that their parents allowed her, but then again, even they were powerless to stop her. Even Azia lacked the power required to stop her.

Turning back to her sister, she made sure she didn't turn away from her gaze… made sure her sister's eyes met hers.

Seeing the fear in Starlis' face, she smiled a cruel and bitter smile. Hooking invisible hooks into her sister's mind, she spoke, do not worry dear sister you will not remember much of this I do promise.

What are you doing? How? This… this is…

Forbidden? Yes, I know. But then again, I have never been one for rules. Now hush and you will know what it is you must do.

I… The hooks drove deeper intertwining with the very fabric of Starlis' mind. Defeated, her body sagged. *What must I do?*

When asked, you will tell our parents I tried to flee and was swept away in the Void. I in a sense died just as those who were foolish enough to try have done since the beginning of time.

Starlis was mortified of what her sister was proposing. *Your powers will never feed the Star City. Our family will have no tribute.*

Actually, it will have two. Since our parents are so keen on the idea of keeping the tradition, they can offer themselves.

Mother's power will pass to you as queen... but father's? Well, he can feed the catacombs of Pallas.

I suppose. I doubt the Azia will check to see who has been offered as tribute.

Primitiva smiled, *I know he will not. Now, my daughter. You will raise her as your own. She will be your child.*

But...

Your only child. Your powers are weak compared to hers and she is only but days old. None outside our parents know I gave birth. And none will think twice about you having a child with no interest in love.

Because my sister can create life out of nothing. Yes, that is plausible.

A New World

So glad you agree since you won't remember much in a few minutes. Now… She stepped back and called in a single tribute box. Silver but the inlays were not that of melting magma, but of shimmering crystal. *This will be passed down in our bloodlines for three generations. That is three thousand years where I am going.*

This box will only open to the first male child born who is the first- born. From now on… for the next three generations, the father of the child will be the tribute. No excuses. This instruction will be passed down to the children of the crown.

I understand.

Calling the mist back to her, she smiled, "No sister, you do not. You do not have the gift of foresight. But that is ok for I do." Wrapping her arms around her sister, she gave her one last hug. "Close your eyes, my dear and I will be gone by the time you open them."

CHAPTER 5: GOVARD

Being the crown prince of any city was bound to have secrets. More then a few. But damn it why did he have to know this one now.

Alright fine. He wasn't a youth but he also wasn't yet old enough to be considered an adult. Yes old enough to find a bride but not old enough to need one.

By the light he was caught somewhere between the two. In the years where he was still free from burden yet was old enough to start learning what it meant to rule. Still, why did his father choose this very day to tell him about his bloodlines? Why had he chosen today to show him the secret that the city held.?

Oh bloody hell. Fine. Time to honest with himself. He was in truth older than most rulers when they ascended. Old enough to have at least one child if held by the standards of any other . Still, he was not ready to know the secrets that his father held. Or at least was not ready to be the crown prince and have that responsibility.

Ok breathe. His father was king and he didn't have to explain his actions to anyone. His mother, OOO his mother the little traitor, held more secrets than any ruler ever could.

A New World

Still there had to be a reason. Had to be at least one reason that he was being pushed into knowing things now.

A deep breath and Govard blew it out slowly. He would be arriving on Nexus soon. Be polite , don't touch anything. And do not get close to them. That had been his mother's warning. The queen however gave a different order, Find the queen she will tell you what you need. Do not ask for things not said.

Cryptic as always but his mother understood the dark stars better than anyone. Actually most royal fey would come to Arcadian just to ask her guidance before entering one of the darker stars. She was trusted for her advice. So he as her son knew the importance of the word of the queen above the word of his mother.

But being the son, he also knew the queen had quietly given misinformation to those who could not be trusted. Those fools would never return to their homes. Nor would any ever find them.

His mother would not allow harm to come to him. His queen however…

Ah!!!

If he kept thinking like that he would never see his home again.

"Stop it Govard. Nexus was your choice." he scolded himself. "You are going to meet the queen. This is a needed trip and neither the king nor queen would send you here if they didn't think you would survive."

He wasn't a coward but maybe he should have seen one of the other star cities first? And what would he have chosen. Each held beauty as it held danger. True the dark stars were the most dangerous but there was danger among all of the stars.

Stepping out of the coach Govard looked around. A desolate wasteland. Abandon stone structures that were being held together by spider-silk. There were no fey walking the crumbling streets. No lights withing the buildings. So where was everyone?

He glanced back at the one who pulled the coach, "Wait here I doubt I'll be gone long."

The man just nodded once.

Not surprising. Most messengers didn't speak unless they had to. Even then it was never more than a few words.

Just something else to ponder but not today.

A New World

Keeping his footing he made his way down the few broken steps and onto the main street. He could feel power here here. Could feel something that warned of life yet for all he could see there was nothing.

Not a single soul. Not even a spider.

"Most curious." he mumbled as he walked the empty streets of could have been a market place.

Turning a corner he stopped suddenly as the cloaked figure stepped out of a hidden cellar. "I mean no intrusion."   He raised he hand just enough to show he held no weapon.

For several breaths neither of them moved. Her long threadbare cloak barely moving with the breeze. Slowly she removed her hood revealing her thin face and long dark hair. "You are the child of Chiara."

Not a question. Yet she sounded curious.

Slowly he took a step forward just to close the gap between them. A single nod, "I am, my name is-"

"Govard. Come the queen is ready to meet you."

"Thank you."

The chamber of the queen was lit in black candles. Red cloth covered the floor. And the walls… Earthen based. Those that dwelled here had no need for light. No need for windows. And less need for basic foods. No they were not only the bringers of death for they were death internals.

Fey that none other could fathom being. Their touch was deadly but only if they so wished it. The source of their powers? Even the greatest of fey could not say. Nor would they dare to guess.

The young woman turned to him, "The queen will be here shortly. I offer you this advice. Keep your distance young prince and **do not** breath a word you hear today to another soul."

Govard watch the woman leave. Who she was or what she had wanted he would never know. Nor did he need to. He was a guest here, at least for the moment. But being a guest didn't mean he would live to return home.

Her steps were quite and unhurried. Drawing closer he could see the dark cloak wasn't black but a faded blue.

Almost gray. Fibers missing. Old or maybe it was fashion he couldn't tell, nor would he ask.

"I am Shivani, queen of Nexus. Why have you come young one?"

Tipping his head in a bow he allowed his eyes to meet hers. "I seek wisdom from a seer."

Shivani let her long narrow finger trace the contour of the wall. Wax from a candle dripping onto her long nail. "Are there no seers within your own home?"

He was being bated but having Chiara as a mother he knew the proper answer. "None I would ask the questions that that I have."

She turned to him and the smile was not the least bit reassuring. "You seek knowledge on where you may find a suitable bride. Yes?"

"That is part of it."

"The bride you seek is not yet born, She will give you a gift that will be needed but not stand beside you on the battlements. Nor will she ever grace the halls of your home."

That didn't make sense. He was the crown prince. There was no reason for him to take a bride who wouldn't return to him home. None.

"Thank you , your majesty for your time… I'll-"

"Sit Govard, I am not yet done with you."

A New World

Chapter 6: Nexus

For several movements after Govard had been taken away She said nothing. She couldn't. The lives of her people meant everything to her, but to back what she knew…

No. Too many lives would be lost if she did nothing.

Kaida. Yes her youngest . that would do nicely. It would protect Nexus but not give too much of a connection to the crown. After all Azia had said only the eldest is worth their weight in riches. The other were only fonder.

But how to prepare her? Kaida was not the most gifted in the gifts of nexus. Not in poisons or giving life to those once dead. No but she had other uses. Perhaps…

"Guards!"

Never in all her years had she summoned her guards to this room. Never had she needed to. So it was no wonder the two that answered her summons looked more confused than battle ready.

No matter she would deal with that shortly. "Bring Kaida here at once. Then summon the army I want them outside within the hour."

A New World

There was warning there. Being outside was only for trading days and when messengers had came. Summoning the army. War was brewing and soon they would all know it.

She was young sinewy built. Her coal black hair braided down to the small of her back. She was a princess , she was a huntress, but more importantly she was a trained assassin. Her father had begun her training with weapons as soon as she could walk. Her mother with poisons before she could form full sentences.

In the last five light cycles she had taken the life of those who had sought to control Nexus. Killed because she had her orders. Orders that came from the queen herself, and orders she would never fail at.

Her fist hit the target dummy yet again. Sleep, train, eat, train, then sleep once more. That was her life. Had always been her life. And as far as she was concerned would always be her life. Nothing would change that.

And flick of cold rage rage ran thru her and her dagger split her dummy in half sending it to the floor with a loud thunk.

"Damn it. Can they not make these inferno things stable enough to handle a blade?" It wasn't said to any one. And in truth there was none there to hear her.

As a princess she was forbidden contact for most days. Meals were delivered on a tray and left for her. Training , learning new things came from either her mother or father. Outside of that if she was socializing it was to learn her mark before taking his or her life. Even then it was her father who told her of her assignment.

"Princess Kaida?"

The sound startled her. The face she knew as one of the queens guards, but the voice. "Well, what is it?"

The guard bowed his head, "The queen has requested you come."

This was wrong, had to be wrong. Her mother didn't send for her, the queen would come here herself. So this was wrong… very wrong. Still he let the guard lead the way.

A New World

Several turns. Her footfalls as quiet as she could make them. Her breathing controlled. Just a training mission. Yes that had to be why they were going into the catacombs.

As they came to the large thick door the guard nodded for her to enter. Not a room that she knew. Not an area that she had ever been taken too. And a room she would never forget.

Chapter 7: Primitiva

Metal clanged as armed guards entered the castle. An angry voice barked orders from inside the heart of the castle. And men argued. All the while Primitiva smiled as she listened. These men had little in the way of wits and much in the way of temper.

Lazily she flipped through the pages of a book that she had found during her exploration of this castle. The castle itself would need to be remade, but what she had found inside… written words… books Alec had called them… those she would keep.

Many of them like this one gave her ideas on what to turn people into. Those who would be her high-born citizens and those who would serve those who belonged to the crown. Of course, some would remain human. She just simply couldn't transform every living person into a beautiful fallen creature…

Well, she could, but why would she?

Feeling her first creations drawing near she smiled. It would figure Nicco would be the first to arrive. Once he reformed into a solid mass he took a knee, "My queen?"

Her fingers run through his black hair, "You are a trouble maker. I see it in your soul."

"Would you have me be something else?"

She shook her head, "After today we will find something suitable for you to do with all your time. But for today… You will not do anything without my approval. Is that understood?"

"Yes, my queen."

"Good. Now stand the others are arriving."

She waited for only a heartbeat before after they came into view before addressing them, "You will remain here until I summon you." She paused letting her gaze settle on Nicco, "Quietly."

"Yes, my queen." They all said in unison.

Pushing the doors to where the former royal family had gathered Primitiva Glided into the room. In an instant, all of the arguing ceased and one of the other kings growled, "Guards cease her."

"Oh come now, do you really wish to play mindless games?"

Quickly the armed guards surrounded her their silver swords held tightly in their hands. "Kneel wrench."

"Kneel? Yes, That sounds like a fabulous idea." With a flick of her hand, all of the guards knelt before her. She gave the others a moment to realize what she was before stepping over the men who no blocked her path. The brother of thing that she had seen last night took a step back in horror. Thinking he was trying to escape the room filled with thunder. Bolts of lighting, blocking every exit. "Now, perhaps I should explain why you are all here."

"You, what are you?"

"Some call me goddess and others Queen. You may call me your grace. I do like the sound of that."

In a breath, he pulled his sword from its hilt and charged at her. Unfazed, she yawned, then he froze, unable to move more than breath and blink. "I think I have had enough of mere humans trying to pull a sword on me." A snap of her fingers and all the swords that were held turned into a puddle of melted silver cooling on the hard stone floor. "There, much better."

Slowly the black mist filled the room and with it the lungs of the human men who had been frozen by her. A few coughed as the mist clogged their throats, others tried not to breathe at all. Useless because there was no way for them to escape the mist. One by one each succumb to her power and helplessly submitted to her orders.

"Now, Those of you who claim to be rulers you will go and address your subjects. All that was yours, you will give to me. You will tell them… " She paused needing to have something plausible to tell the citizens so they would not fear her but also do as she told them. Turning, she let the heavy doors once again open, "My darlings, please enter I am in need of your counsel."

Their eyes barely scanned the room before they kneeled, "How may we be of service, Goddess?"

"You know the human race… What should be told to them so they will follow my orders and not try to harm me?" Not that any of them could but why shed their blood if she didn't need to?

As the scribe, Karnack slowly approached as he said, "I may have a suggestion, my queen."

"Ah yes, please enlighten me?"

"Since you are a goddess, perhaps you should play into it. You fell from the sky to deliver them from these worthless creatures who have controlled them for far too long?"

"Ah yes, that does sound about right." Turning back to her captives, "You will tell those who live within your realms that a goddess has come to your realm. She is displeased with how her children have been treated and is here to take back what had been created so many millennia back. Then will introduce me as the goddess Primitiva."

A day later King Gregor stepped foot onto his balcony of burnt stone. "People of Westernesse stand before me, your king."

Slowly the city square started to fill with people. No-one making so much as a single murmur of speculation about whatever the announcement could be. None daring to look directly at the king but at the castle walls that stood before them.

"As king, it is my sole job to see to the comfort and discipline of you, my children. But is would seem one thinks that I do not take pride in my responsibility and has come to take back what is rightfully theirs."

The crowd gasped. How would be so foolish to challenge the king?

A New World

"After speaking to this person, it would appear that they are right and I have no recourse but to give them my throne and this kingdom. Please welcome the Goddess Primitiva." He didn't step aside, but looked into the sky to the silver dragon that was lazily gliding down to the castle walls.

As it landed just above the balcony on the castle walls she glided gown the few feet to where the now former king stood. "Citizens of… what did you call this place again?"

"Westernesse, Goddess."

"Westernesse? What a horrible name for a city. As of this moment, this city will be called Night. This shall be the largest city in is now my realm."

Slowly the citizens began to kneel understanding the woman who stood before them now was more menacing than the king that they had been just dispatched before their eyes.

"To show you my powers let us being with this creature who called himself a king." She turned to face him, letting him see a cruel smile form on her lips. "You are an abomination of flesh and I do not grant you a gift. Instead, I grant you a life of a monster so hideous that you are only to be kept in the mines working until the day you no longer draw breath. Leave the mines and you become food for my darlings."

Not waiting for him to reply a brown and green mist overtook him. The sound of bones snapping echoed throughout the city square as his screams turned to the growling snapping of jaws.

When the mist subsided He stood nearly twice her height. His skin, thick with slim now the color of pond muck. Only four teeth remaining in his mouth and those overgrown and pointed. Only his eyes were left untouched.

"Any who diss obey me will be turned into a troll and enslaved in the mines searching for treasures. The rest of you know this those who serve me well will be rewarded with kindness and possibly a life much better than most. Those who wish not to become one of my favorites… do so at your own discretion. I will not waste my gifts on those who don't deserve them.

A New World

Chapter 8: Pallas

Soon his child would be born. The seers all confirmed it would be a strong boy. Once that would rule far beyond the lights of Pallas. A boy strong enough to face anything that may stand in his way. A son he could be proud of .

Teaching him what it meant to rule all of the stars would be his greatest accompaniment. Well second. The first was ridding the stars long ago of his brother. Bah! Why would Pallas need a general who was more glorious than it's King?

Blasted Mabuz. They could have conquered the outer cities. The ones that still didn't stand in the shadow of Pallas. But , NOOO the bastard wanted to be known on all of the stars. Known as the true leader of Pallas while he the Azia only profited from his labor.

The blade had gone thru him to quickly and the look on his face. Oh the look of shock and horror. Just as well he lived long enough to see the same blade slice cleanly thru their parents as well.

Azia sat back and laughed as he drank his honeyed nectar remembering the day he had shown the rulers of the stars what it would mean to stand against him. His mother had lived long enough to have the dirt of the garden cover her. She had tried to fight the blood loss while clawing her way out of the grave. She died just as her hand broke free of the ground.

He had honored her by leaving the hand to rot in the sun. The carrion eaters picking the flesh from the bone. Later he left a little statue of a skeleton hand at the base the inscription here lays the traitor queen of Pallas.

In all of his years since, she had been the only one to claw their way to the surface. No between the death wounds and the ground soaking up their energy none had been successful. Nor will any ever be.

The door to the dinning hall opened but it wasn't a servant carrying another bottle of nectar but rather one of the royal guards carrying some contraption.

"My grace?"

Sitting up within his chair he glared at the man, the armor pristine. The words spoken properly. "Well what is it?"

"A messenger brought this. He said it's a message from a star city."

"Hmp. Probably Arcadian. The damn star all seem to think these contraptions are better then parchment and quill."

"The messenger reeked of dark power. Arcadianians reek of metal and sweat."

"Leave it. I'll deal with barter between the cities another day."

He made sure the guard was long gone before handling the small device. Nothing really marvelous about it. Small enough to fit in his hand. An octagon with a crystal on the top. "Well how to I make the dam thing work."

He had no longer spoken as an apparition was seated at the table next to him. "Still so short sided I see."

Falling from his seat Azia scrambled back to the table. "No, it can't be you're dead."

The apparition leaned in just a hair. "Dead? You don't sound so certain of that, brother. But no matter. I was asked to deliver a message to you. What you do is up to you, the great Azia."

Snarling Azia took his seat, until this bit of craft was done he wouldn't find out anything useful. And he couldn't kill the general for a second time. "And what message can a specter give me that my advisors can't?"

Mabuz smiled, "I pray for the day I see you on the battlefield brother. I pray for the day I can drag your lifeless body to the field and feed it to the Arae. But my queen leaves you a gift The castle of Akrsna now stand in the shadow of Pallas. May it's dark halls be for your will."

A New World

Before Azia could respond a nursemaid ran into the room. "Your grace?"

The specter forgotten, "The child?"

The young woman gazed at the ground, "Stillborn your grace."

He threw the pitcher across the room spilling the contents as it flew. "Damn it. Why can't these wenches manage to do one thing right?" He paused, "Take the mother to the square and kill her. I will not feed a worthless bottom feeder."

CHAPTER 9: ARKRSNA

Aanshi sat quietly watching Mabuz. She could hear how he spoke but not the answers Azia was giving. So she stayed silent until he closed his eyes and closed the crystal lid . "General?" What else could she call him? What else would she dare until she had answers.

"Prepare the citizens to leave the city. We can't wait any longer."

"I have been the queen here and it pains me to surrender."

A smile twitched upon his lips, "We are not surrendering my love and one day we will return to our home. Even if I have to tear every brick from the castle and rebuild it."

"I will hold you to that."

"Aye, as I know you will." Slowly he got up and took her hand, kissing her fingers softly he added, "We have been long away from our youngest I pry it's time to teach her what she'll need."

A New World

The halls were empty. The citizens gone. All scattered across the void and held within the stars that she could trust. Soon would come the day when word would spread for them to feed the void. And darkness would take root within the royals.

Darkness and the lust for blood. Everything that went against the nature of true Fay would be called into question. Everything that went against Azia would be met with death.

Her finger caressed the wall of her private sanctum. The woman standing before her not one she knew. So young. So beautiful. The red hair and the fire of the dragon running within her blood.

Oh she wouldn't save the stars but she would the symbol that would rally the troops when the time came.

"My love?"

"We need to buy her time. And we will need to send her a gift."

Mabuz leaned against the door frame not daring to enter, "What kind of gift?"

She turned to him tears in her eyes. "One that will save the fey."

He hadn't pressed her on what all she saw. He didn't need to. Sometimes what was seen never came to pass. But other times what was seen could never be stopped. So instead as they sat alone in the coach that would take them into hiding he asked, "What do you think Azia will do finding the star abandoned?"

She took a shaky breath, "Our home will become a living testament to those who oppose him. The scrolls left tell of the Arae and her power. It tells of the item that will call her forth. His lust for power will have him stopping at nothing to find what he seeks."

"Akrsna doesn't work like other stars. For some it drains their energy and for others gives them strength. Azia may end up making the one that will be his undoing."

A New World

Her hand was steady when she placed it on his face. "No, your brother will never meet Arae . But there will be a time and place she will be needed."

Pulling her close Mabuz held his love, his wife until her was sure she was no longer shaking, "If she will be needed , lets see what we can do to prolong that day for as long as possible."

Chapter 10: Arcadian

It felt like forever since he had left his home. Left to visit the other star cities. Left to find a bride. And the more he thought about it the less he wanted a bride and the more he just wanted to be home.

The queen of Nexus had told him what he needed to hear. Oh most of what she said, he was still trying to understand. Most he didn't think that he ever would. But that was something to think about at another time.

No the more pressing matter was how the other star cities lived. Not the royals but the citizens. So many lived in poverty and looked barely alive. Those near the cites? Those were fey, borne and bread for battles.   From their homes to their armor, there were ready for any fight.

Sadly he didn't think any of them would live long enough to see the winner should there be a real battle. After all you can not just use your natural ability in a fight. All fey have magic, and power. They all have a natural ability but to only use it in battle was suicide.

Just plain suicide.

Idiots. Fools,

And for the royals not to see it. Bah! They were just as blind.

A New World

The armies needed weapons. They needed armor that would protect them and their homes not just look shiny.

Govard took a deep breath. It was not his job, his duty to make the other royals do what was best for their homes. It was however, his job to what was best for his people. His kingdom.

His…

The shock of the word rocked him. His… the kingdom and it's people were his father's not his. Yet , one day they would be and the current kind did listen to him. Would listen to him even if they had to express what was needed as loud as they could.

Stepping out the coach he looked around the streets were packed with people. Too many people. Their clothes all not from around here.

He wasn't gone that long, had he?

"Citizens of Akrsna please head to the conventions center for registration. Those with Dark abilities please follow the black line to re-homing."

The voice boomed across the communications hubs. What the … " His eyes scanned the sea of people. None looked worried but there was a sense of urgency in their movements. Not fear so what was causing…

"Your highness you return was not expected until next week."

Older voice. Kind. Not an enemy but right now that was what was pricking his skin. Enemy. Danger.

The sound around him faded into a deafening silence and he tuned everything and everyone out. His senses nearly honed for battle yet there was no worthy opponent. At least not one he could see.

But they were here. He could feel it.

"Govard!"

A New World

A voice called to him. Dark and commanding. A voice he knew.

"Stand down."

Stand down? The voice wanted him to stand down? He was surrounded by those who were snakes seeped in the flesh of fey.

" Govard al Arcadian, Stand DOWN!"

That voice demanded a response. That was a voice he knew. His eyes slowly focused to where the sound came from. There not far from him was his mother.

OOOOH No, the look on her face she was not here as his mother, she here as the queen of Arcadian. A deep breath and he gave her his best boy hood smile that he could. "Yes you're grace?" he asked meekly.

She blew out a breath. "Castle. Now."

Shit he was in trouble. Too bad he didn't know why.

No that wasn't true. He was reacting to something here. Something he would have to identify before he did something to truly have his mother's wrath.

Nodding once he made his way thru the streets. Weaving in and out of families that were from too many cities for this to be a normal celebration.

Something was going here , he just wished he knew what "it" was .

Arcadian guards were stationed along the outer wall of the castle grounds. Turrets he corrected scanning the crowds. Watching everything yet not seeing what was before him , Govard let out an audible, "UMP." as he bumped into someone leaving the castle.

"Abdou?"

The forge master looked him up and down. "When you're done with your father, come to the forge."

Nodding once he allowed the man to pass noticing one of the sentries making his way toward him. His eyes warned caution but the face was one that he knew, "Talos? What is going on here?"

"I have orders to escort you to the throne room."

Stoic, professional tone. Words said for the benefit of others. Yet.. as they entered the castle it wasn't the direction of the throne room they were taking.

A New World

Passing an alcove Govard stopped and grabbed his friend's arm, "Want to tell me what's really going on."

"The rulers of Akrsna arrived days after you left. Then the other started coming. They are fleeing their homes but from what or why…" Talos paused, "a few are fighters but most are woman with small children. Non of those here are from cities that are known to Pallas."

"So why are they here?"

Two thousand years before the Great War.

"We have sent our strong to an ally . A friend who the seers all trust. Yet they speak of the destruction that is yet to come. We must survive. We must.

This war is not ours to fight. But our blood will be needed to hold the evil back."

- Unknown ruler of Flyta

A New World

CHAPTER 11: PALLAS

The snifter that he just fill flew across the room landing in the hearth. The blue flames raging up for only a moment. The rage within those flames matching his mood.

With each light cycle that had passed his son has been born , he had found new ways to give thanks to the void. Filling it more worthless fey than any ruler before.

Letting their lifeless bodies float in the endless space creating a cesspool of untapped power. First born royals and lowly servants just the same.

All of them feeding their power into Pallas. Oh, it was said they were feeding the Void, but in reality they were feeding the great star of Pallas. They were feeding the flora and fauna. Feeding the very essence of the fey.

Magmas the fool was becoming a problem. Letting Avyanna kill those sniveling brats should have curb their father's thought of leading a revolt.

It hadn't.

What more could he do to teach these fools a lesson?

A New World

The idea formed before he could stop it. Why stop at one star city? Why wait for the stars to align and come for him? He was Azia. He was the ruler of all of the known stars.

His lips twitched into an evil smile.

Yes…

… Yes

"YES!" he yelled into the empty room. Getting to his feet, "Guards!"

The two sentries rushed in. Their eyes wary yet they stood ready to answer anything thing that Azia needed.

"Get the armies ready. The stars will bow at my feet."

Chapter 14: Arcadian

"Arcadian is for now a safe haven for the fey who need to hide. We have the room Govard. And we have a duty to train those here to use our defenses."

He paced the confines of not the throne room but some hidey hole well beneath the palace. Some room hidden in the labyrinth his father had built so long ago. *"I'm not saying turn our back on the fey but, why here?"*

Daedalus took a breath and placed his hands on Govard's shoulders making him stand still and look him in the eye. *"You are my son and I will always have a duty to protect you. But I am also king and I also have a duty to aid those to ask for help."*

"I know... but.."

"But nothing. You visited the dark stars and spoke to the seers."

Shit that should have been a secret. *"I did."*

"And they all said your place is not here but it is here."

Nodding Govard whispered, *"They also said my bride is not yet born nor is on a star known to Pallas."*

A New World

Daedalus smiled, *"Well maybe you will find someone here to keep you occupied for a spell."*

"Or I could just continue work on the battlements."

His father nodded then looked somber. *"The seers that are here all see a threat. There will come a day when you will need to trust, and do as you are told without hesitation. Even if it mean giving your life."*

"Father?"

"Govard, listen carefully. The secrets of Arcadian will remain with you. Always. But you have to trust me."

It had been several light cycles since his father had said those words to him. And never once had they been repeated…

… until now.

Fighting had broken out within the city. Loud explosions that were getting closer. Too many people yelling. Somewhere children were crying.

This is what he had been awaken to. No time to dress. No time for anything before the door of his bed chamber crashed open and his father rushed in.

"You have to go." He looked exhausted and worried, in a state of dress. His leather trousers barely fastened with his sword gripped in his hand.

"Father?" he said as he quickly got out of bed and crammed his legs into his leather pants.

"Govard. Now. The Void . You must go."

The void? His father meant take a coach because surly he didn't mean... "You want me to..."

Daedalus turned from the door. "Govard, listen to me. We don't have time. You must do this. Trust me."

He took a breath then nodded. He had promised he would trust his father. Promise he would have faith even if the request meant his life.

There was no time to help his people fight this oncoming army. No time to save the helpless from being slaughtered. Bloody hell, there were too many to even get a clear look at their faces before he let his blade slice thru one before the next attacked.

Who had sent these men here? Why?

No, those answers in time. Those answers if he survived… if…

The messenger's gate was just ahead. A few yards at most.

Govard turned for just a moment. Explosions. Fire. Dark shadows of the enemy coming from every direction. This didn't make sense how had they gotten here. How?

Messengers brought both people and citizen by carriages. But those carriages only held maybe five or six adult fey. This was an army. An invading force.

"Govard! Run!"

His eyes searched for the voice for only heartbeat. Just quick enough to see Talos running to join him. Just in time to see Abdou be run thru with a blade from the enemy.

He stood there in shock. Screaming at the massacre going on around him. "NOOOO!!!" he took a step forward only to have his arm grabbed and pulled the other direction.

"Let go!"

Talos swung him into rubble that might have been a home just a day before. "Your highness, we must go. The secrets of Arcadian rest with you. We.Must Go."

He took a breath.Tears in his eyes knowing Arcadian would fall on this day. Knowing there was nothing he could do to stop what was coming.

Nodding once he agreed.

They stood at the edge of the messengers gate. Looked back as the enemy approached. Not long now. A few breaths maybe less.

"Tell me Talos who sent this army."

"Pallas."

That was all he needed to say. Die here and some dark fay could give him a second life. Pallas would extract every ounce of knowledge he had then kill him. And that death would be anything but kind.

A New World

No the only way to protect his people now was…

"JUMP!"

One jump. One last breath. The cold sliced thru him as his blood froze. Before his world went dark his last thoughts was how this saved his people.

CHAPTER 13: PRIMITIVA

Primitiva gazed out of her solaris window watching the magma bubble up from the riverbed. She heard his light footfalls coming down the long hallway but didn't turn until he gave a hesitant cough. "Alec? Are the boys settled for the moment?"

"They are." Carefully he took a single step into the room.

This was one of her private rooms and not a place that she would normally choose to have anyone for any reason. Yet he had to give her his report on the boys. "They seem younger than they did when you brought them here."

Another bubbled popped as she sighed, "As they should.

Magmas used an incantation on both of them to help hide who was   older. Apollo is barely fifty light cycles. His brother just a few less. From what they both remember their youngest brother has just had   his tenth light cycle… but looks much older."

"Light cycle?" He sounded puzzled. And Alec was rarely puzzled. Yet she had never explained life within the Star Cities. Now it seemed that she would have to.

A New World

Her eyes narrowed into tiny slits as she thought about what she would say. In a thousand years she had been able   to refrain from speaking too much about her home… now? Did she really have a choice? "Each star has a different measurement for light cycles. Those closest to Pallas come into… um… adult form more quickly than those further away. It has something to do with the tributes and how the power is divided between the Star Cities. I know not how it truly works. Some things are forbidden to ask about. And my life is much too important to be killed, asking a silly question."

She heard him shift his weight from foot to foot, unsure of   what to ask. Hear his deep breath just before he asked, "So the boys…"

"Since they're no longer bound to their Star City or to the power that fed the incantation their true forms are becoming apparent. In another day or two, their forced memories will fade and their true one will surface."

Alec slid closer to her, but not yet daring to be close enough to touch. "I don't recall you going through this change."

A soft smile twitched her lips, "I didn't. The moment that I could I broke the bond while still within my home. My parents were not happy. I think my father was punished because he is the one who told me how it could be done." She took a breath and turned back to her window. After several long minutes, she shuddered, "In my Star City the queen and all of the women there have all the power. Or at least are the ones allowed to use the majority of those powers. Most women control every aspect of a man's life. In my father's case with him being the consort, punishment meant pain.

My mother relished in it. I remember days where my father could barely stand even if no wounds were visible. Her pets faired far worse. At one time she had three, only one was still alive when I came here. The other two? Were killed some time before. I assure you their deaths were the only measure of kindness that they ever knew."

"I don't understand." And he didn't. If someone did something that needed punished, they were brought to Prim for judgment. There had only ever been one case where a person was punished in a way that caused pain. Only one in over a thousand years.

"No, I don't suppose you would. I try not to rule the way that is done within the Star Cities. I do not take joy in causing pain.

Although if I had to I would have no problem doing so. No Fey does."

He needed to turn her thoughts before she either harmed herself or something around her. Just standing several feet away, he could feel the heat rising from her now milky white skin. Could see her hair changing at the tips to embers. "Is that why you came here to show them what is possible?"

"I came here so I would not marry Magmas. I was barely what humans refer to as a teenager. I knew not of what I wanted. And In truth, I still don't, But my heart still belongs to me and that counts for something." Another deep breath she cast aside all her thoughts about her home. There were more pressing matters that needed to be taken care of. "Please notify all of the villages both big and small… on moments notice all children must be taken to the nearest castle. They will be housed there until whatever trouble arises has been dealt with."

"You have already notified the other castles…"

"My darling, Do you think I would tell you before I had already made plans for the children? When the castles were built, I had several floors placed well below the surface. Karnack knows of these places since his work rooms are in the lowermost …um… floor seems wrong as does cellar. If this was a Star City it would be below the catacombs… as such I no word for the place."

It was good to see his goddess slowly returning to her normal behavior, "Then I will help you come up with a name for this place of safety."

"As you wish. My mind is too full of other things right now."

Alec bowed his head slightly, "Is there anything you need before I see to the preparations?"

Suddenly the red gem appeared in her hands. "No. I need quite as I find out how to make this cursed thing work in order to speak with Magmas."

Pausing Alec let his eyes lock on the gem that now rested in his queen's hand. Then very hesitantly asked, "Are you sure that is a good idea?"

"No. But he sent his boys here for a reason. I wish to find out why before I decide on what I will do with them."

It didn't take long for her to figure out how to use the seer's stone to look at the other Star Cities… but much longer, not only to find the one that belonged to Magmas but to also figure out how use it to communicate with him. Actually, it wasn't until he was holding the mate to it that he even came into view. Trying only once she softly spoke, "Magmas?"

His eyes, which had been filled with grief, lit up with hope and relief, "I knew you would figure it out." A moment to pause then he whispered, "My boys?"

"Sleeping. Your incantation is fading. I suspect I will have to deal with adolescent questions in the marrow."

A New World

Magmas closed his dull lava red eyes. "Can… when you think it's right… tell them that Flint didn't survive." His face tightened with anger, "Azia had the gall to tell me that none of my current line has the power to rule. As far as he knows he killed all those who could have ruled my Star City."

Seeing the rage building within his eyes, Prim hissed, "Magmas. You need to calm down lest someone hears you."

"I am in the private room known only to the one that rules.

Not even Azia has the power to see within these walls."

Primitiva rolled her eyes as she took a measured breath, "Very well. Your boy. The young one. He has been sent to the catacombs?"

"No. Azia doesn't want him and had forbidden him to feed the ones here. He is to be thrown into the Void. However, I have decided to place him in the ancient catacombs of the first Fey. They have not been used in years, but I…" He let the rest trail off.

For a long moment, she didn't speak. It was a simple gesture, but would he accept it? "I can retrieve his body and bring it here. I make no promises, but I can find something honorable to do with the prince of Osiris."

His through clogged with deep emotions, "I-I would… Thank

you."

"If you can send what you need for me to know. And

Magmas know this if you betray me, I will destroy your Star City and everything in it."

"My sweet, you are my only hope of destroying Azia… why would I ever betray you? I will write down everything you need to know not only about my boys, but the on goings of the Star Cities. War is brewing but it is still sometime a ways."

When the image of Magmas faded, Primitiva sat back on her solaris floor. If what Mamas said was right then she had time to prepare. And possibly do something to help the Star Cities in the process. But she would have to wait until she read what Magmas chose to tell her. What he didn't would prove more valuable than what he did.

A New World

Making her ways outside to the main courtyard, she called for her darling Shesha then waited for the great dragon to appear. She smiled as he came into view. Just a streak of white on a starless night sky.

Back winging as he landed his head bowed slightly, "My queen?"

Coming up to Shesha's side, she stroked his neck lovingly.

So, few were easy around her beloved dragon. Something he never seemed to mind. Today that didn't matter. Getting to where she needed to be quickly… did. "Come, I am in need of your speed."

Shesha bobbled his head in his way of showing her respect. "Of course. Shall I take you to your meadows?"

Climbing up, Primitiva sat petting his long scaly back. "Not today. Do you remember when I told you about my homeland?"

He snorted out a cloud of white smoke. "The balls of light that light the night sky?"

"Yes. We need to go there now. There is one that I seek. We must find him before he enters the outer rim of Pallas."

"Pallas?" The word said more to test how it sounded rather than asking where.

Pointing not to the glowing ball of fire that lights the daytime sky, but rather the large white orb that was currently resting in its shadow. "The great ball of light that glows even during the day."

"Very well, I shall take you there."

Chapter 14: Magmas

Carefully Magmas lifted his son's lifeless body off of the stone platform where he had been placed so that he could be made ready to be laid with the first Fey of their little star. Holding his son close to him, he let a single tear roll down his face. Why had it come to this?

Why?

The Azia had taken to power longer than anyone could remember. In all that time he had never been this cruel. This destructive. He had never killed an entire royal line. So why now?

For a moment longer he sat there collecting not only his thoughts but his emotions. If anyone saw him this way Azia could kill him as well. And if he did, he would find Prim.

Laying his son back down on the cold stone slab Magmas forced himself to go upstairs. He hated what he was about to do, but it needed to be done. If only to protect Prim and to buy himself some much needed time.

Finding the first guard that he came across he carefully spoke. The lad that use to play with Flint and was known to trade identities with him." The guard raised an eyebrow, "Bring him to me.

He is to join Flint in the catacombs. I have no use for someone who has my son's looks within my city."

The guard swallowed, "Of course, my lord. I will retrieve him at once."

Making his way to his children's room, he looked around. Empty shelves lined the walls. Nothing of his children remained within the walls. Flits belongings were already packed and being stored with his body. Prim would find something to do with them, but what she needed now…

… What he needed to do was give Primitiva was a reason to do more.

His fingers ran across the slag wall as he made his way to his private room. Every castle had a room like this. One that no seer could gaze into. A room that was solice for the royal who ruled. Most housed their most prized possessions here. He, on the other hand, housed his maps of the other Star Cities. Housed his notes about what royal Fey ruled each of the known stars. Notes on what royal

Fey had an excess of children. One to rule. One to be sacrificed and the rest to be sold.

Carefully, he placed the maps into a large bag that he could attach to Flint's body. A careful spell would keep him from drifting too far away from their star until Prim found him. This had to work.Taking a seat at his desk, he glanced over at the Seer's eye, tempted to call out to Prim once more. But he shook off the thought. Instead, he took to writing everything that he knew as truth, since she dove into the abyss.

From his visit to tell the Azia about her dishonoring her family to his objecting to Azia raising her daughter. He left nothing out. Not his feeling of betrayal when the Azia killed his wife and all of his pets. Not the rage of losing his children. Not even his plan to remove the Azia from power.

It was a risk telling her that much. A risk that she may decide to side with Azia for the sake of her daughter, but was a risk he was willing to take. After all, it would only be his life that would be affected. However, if she sided with him… or at the very least swore to house the children of the royal Fey that needed to survive in order to rule… that would be more than worth the risk.

Carefully folding the parchment he placed it in the sack with the maps… This had to work or his children had died in vain.

A New World

"The boy is waiting in the hall of tribute, my lord."

Magmas paused, seeing the grief hidden in the guard's eyes.

He knew too well what that grief meant. "Your son will forever be with the prince, he served deep within the royal tomb. It is a great honor."

The guard nodded once and turned. Not surprising when he was king and he could require anything from his subjects including their deaths. He hated that his citizens blindly followed his command, but right now he was also thankful.

Slipping into the throne room, he saw the boy standing alone facing the door. Fear in his eyes. "What did your father tell you?"

"It is a great privilege to be forever linked with the prince."

If he sounded any more grateful tears would be pouring from his eyes. "I swear you will not feel a thing."

"May I speak plainly?"

As he would be dead in the next few moments Magmas nodded for the boy to speak.

"It's not the pain that fear. It's the loss of all that I will never get to do."

Going down on one knee, he smiled, "What you will be doing is far greater than anything you could have done otherwise. Now, please follow me. I do not think it wise to delay what is to come."

"Yes, sir."

Letting the lad walk in front of him, they entered a stark, dimly lit room. Not a single piece of furniture. Nor anything to offer even a glimmer of hope. The boy paused as he took his first step into the room. Then made a move as if he was going to turn around. In one quick motion, Magmas snapped his neck, saving him any pain that he might have felt otherwise.

A New World

Closing his eyes, he prayed to the gods that he had made the correct decision. Prayed that he didn't take this life without cause. But most of all he prayed that the boy had the strength that Flint had so the deception would not ever be discovered.

Carefully, he lifted the boy's body from the floor and carried it to where his own son laid. Then began the slow painful task of dressing the boy in a similar fashion. Long robes bearing the colors of royalty. A small incision on the neck and a vine of mist forced all of the blood… hunter green blood… from the boy's body. Allowing it to pool onto the floor below the body.

In the morning the body would be moved to the ancient catacombs. Laid on a shelf with the ancestors. Laid forever in slumber with the first Fey of Osiris. No one would ever know the difference. The slit on the throat would be seen as a father's act of anger that his offspring had died so shortly after being made the crown prince.

It was a reasonable explanation.

Waiting until the halls of the castle were quiet and the city was bedded down for the night, Magmas carried his son's body to the messenger's platform. He had stowed the heavy bags here earlier knowing none would care to disturb the bags nor care to glimpse inside.

Securing the packs to Flint's lifeless body, he held on for a moment longer. Held on wishing for only one minute more with his youngest. One minute for with any of his children. Before he could change his mind about sending his son's body away, he let his body fall from his arms and into the Void. He watched as his son's body floated away from the platform. Watched as the pack that held his belonging pulled slightly from his limp body.

Primitiva would find him. She had to. Not that she could do anything to help him… except give him a final resting place due to any royal Fey. His now crown prince.

Magmas closed his lava red eyes so not to allow them to fill with the tears that were held deep inside him. He could not appear weak. He couldn't. Prim's life would be lost if he did.

Then again, if anyone ever found out that Prim had taken the body or that she was somehow still alive…

Closing his eyes, he took a deep, controlled breath. He had to keep the appearances of indifference. He needed to look like he didn't care that his children… all of them… were gone. Even the Void couldn't touch them now. Another breath. He would need to sire another child to prove his indifference.

He just hoped that child would survive what was coming.

Deep down, he didn't think that hope would be answered.

Of course, if Prim actually helped the Star Cities... War could be avoided altogether. But this was something she wouldn't do.

She had no desire to rule the Fey. She didn't want more than she had created on her little blue star.

No. The only help she would offer was a place to hide the children of the royal Fey. The ones that were strong enough to rule. Yet too young to do so. And she would only do so if she star was never found. That was her only term and one that was not negotiable.

Slowly he turned away from the platform. Tonight, he would grieve the loss of his youngest. Then tomorrow he would carefully see which Star Cities grew tired of the Azia and who would follow him till their last breath.

With his long red robe trailing behind him Magmas took his first step into his palace since the Azia had left. The first since his sons were no longer there. The first step and utter silence surrounded him. He had no wife as of now. No concubine to amuse him. And no children to detract him from all that had happened in a mere few days.

How could one live like this?

His people were content to live by themselves until it was time to take a mate. And he knew lots of other royal Fey that sent their crown prince or princess away to grow on Pallas until it was time for them to rule. Yet how did they manage the silence? It was deafening.

He needed to either start his way to the other Star Cities seeing who could be trusted or start looking for a wife. Neither sounded palatable right now. The thought of becoming a father again turned his stomach. The knowledge of why he would be traveling to the other Star Cities felt far worse.

One of his maids scurried past trying to stay in the shadows… trying not to draw his attention nor his wrath. Or possible, trying not to change her position from maid to bed warmer.

As he turned away from her he made sure she understood he was not looking in her direction. Least not yet. As of today, he was not that desperate to have a common house Fey warming his bed. No even today he had standards and only a royal Fey would do. Only a royal Fey would be worthy of the title of wife.

Luckily, he knew a few Star Cities that had an abundance of royal Fey children and all ripe to be married for a sake of an alliance. And it would make no difference if the child would become a first wife, a concubine, or just a pet. No, the only thing that would matter would be if he kept the child alive.

Chapter 15: Primitiva

As she flew higher the air became colder and dark. Soon she could see her blue star with a clarity that she hadn't seen before. Breathtakingly lovely, but she was not here to take in the rare beauty of her little star. No, she had to find the last of Magmas' line; she had to find his youngest son. If only she knew where to look.

Sitting on Shesha's back, she stroked his long spines soothingly. Her eyes already focusing on each of the stars still thousands of miles away. Osiris was known for its violent volcanoes and lava baths. Even if she had never seen them herself, she had heard about them. So, with that much heat, the star had to be close to Pallas. That narrowed it down to about a hundred stars. Perhaps even a few more.

Patting Shesha she pointed, "That way. Head toward the bright ball of light and quickly. The pull of Pallas is much greater than any other."

He spiraled toward the requested ball. His wings pumping furiously trying to gain as much speed as he could. This was his first time in what his queen called the Void. A place where the air was barely tolerable. A place leached from all light except that of her Star Cities. A place he did not wish to return to ever again. Still, his queen requested his speed and strength for this one mission. Finding every bit of strength that he could, he pushed further into the Void.

"There. Over there." Prim pointed to a lone something floating yet not being pulled toward anything. As they drew closer she could see two large packs attached to the body. Almost upon it, she could see it was a truly lifeless body clad in the robes of a crown prince.

Flint. They had found him. Shesha stopped just close enough for Prim to pull the body to his back. "We are too late?" He asked, his voice full of mourning.

"I…" She paused combing her fingers through his blood matted hair. "… No. He is not so far gone that I can grant him a full life."

Shesha turned to head home, then heard a loud sobbing gasp from his queen, "My lady?"

It was then she saw everything else. Saw the lifeless bodies from too many Star Cities floating motionless withing the Void.

"Look at them. All of them. Why…" A tear ran down her face as she gasped out, "What is Azia doing to the Fey? He will surely kill them all."

"My queen." He paused, seeing now the hundreds of bodies mindlessly floating between the Star Cities. Carnage even he could not fathom. "Should we help them?"

Prim scrubbed her hands over her face. A few more sniffles to calm herself, then she quickly pulled herself together. Her only thought was what was coming and the choices she would need to make. Most more difficult than this one. "We must. If anything they will be highly trained warriors that will be needed for what is to come."

Slowly and cautiously she stood on her great beast's back and closed her eyes. Carefully, she felt for each of the lifeless bodies. Nearly a hundred close to Pallas alone. From where Shesha had brought her, she could feel thousands of them.

Possibly more that were too far from where she was to feel.

A thin string of light no bigger than that of a spider's web attached to each of the bodies. Quickly she attached the string to Shesha's massive tail. "Go further into the Void. I wish to make sure I have all of those that I can."

The further away from the giant ball of light that they went the fewer bodies they found. "I do not see any more, my queen."

"Then the gods are in our favor. Let us return to our home."

A hesitant pause from her favorite. From the King of the dragons. "Where should we take them, my queen?"

A New World

That was the question, wasn't it? So many from different skills and different abilities. All of them would be needed when the war truly started. But for now, what could she do? Taking a deep shaking voice, she made her choice. The only real choice as far as she was concerned. "I will manually drain them into the healing river, it is the only place large enough that will accommodate this many at once. I will decide after they are whole once more, what I will do with them."

Shesha bobbed his head in agreement, "You are wise my queen."

Tens of thousands of bodies drifted in the river. Bouncing off of each other as the current flowed downstream. Each only partly attached to the river bed so not to float way completely. Royal Fey. Common Fey. Fey that was born little more than a slave all of them now mixing together within the warm waters, unaware of who it was they were floating next to. Unaware of their blood mixing with those of lesser rank.

Their blood floating on the top of the waters. Royal blue… Forest green… Lightning yellow… Earthy brown… Lava red… Smoke black. All of it swirling around covering every space that was not occupied by the fallen Fey.

For a long moment, Prim hovered high above the healing river watching the bodies bump into one another. Watching the rivers seep away the abilities of those who now rested within its waters. Knowing that the abilities that were now being taken away would forever feed the lands of her little star. Knowing those abilities would once again be reclaimed in the years that would follow. Knowing that once reclaimed so too would a better understanding of how to use those abilities.

Her eyes swept over the banks of the river. She needed to decide what she was going to. The Eostre were all there. Proud warriors standing keeping watch over those whom she had brought to their lands. Their eyes looking for any sign of life. Looking for any signs of trouble.

More Eostre were there creeping along the river bed and clinging to the trees. A fine black mist where no shadow should be was the only sign of them. The only sign they were seeing if they could devour the lifeless bodies.

Closing her grief filled eyes, she touched each of the fallen Fey. She never wanted this. Never wanted to rule over actual Fey. Never dreamed of living on a star with so many… all with different talents and abilities. All born for different reasons. No, she didn't want this, but what she wanted no longer mattered. They didn't deserve to die like this. To die unrecognized for their talents.

A New World

Unrecognized for their power. Not they didn't deserve this.

She just hoped they would come to see her as her creations saw her and not someone to be feared. But most of all she prayed they would be the strength that she needed to keep her little star safe.

By the gods, how she prayed.

In one quick motion, the bodies sank to the riverbed. The waters already tainted and cloudy with their blood. Gone was the translucent waters replaced by the blood that had been steadily draining from their bodies. One day the water would become clear once more…

… Hopefully…

Thin strings of bright light touched each of the Fey. Touched each of their minds… their hearts. Before reviving them, she forced a simple truth into each. They had been dishonored in death. Dishonored on their own Star City. Their bodies tossed into the Void to be swallowed up and destroyed. Their abilities and powers not worthy of feeding even the most pitiful of catacombs. Not worthy of feeding their own Star City or that of any other. She the creator of life found them and took mercy on each of them.

Granting each a second chance to prove their loyalty. She granted them a second life and she could take her gift back, leaving nothing of them but a memory.

Slowly she withdrew each of her strands of light and allowed for each of the fallen to claw their way out of the water. Each gasped as their heads found air. Each coughed and gasped loudly as they found dry land. When their eyes found the sentries stand over them, none dared to move.

As the last Fey climbed from the water Prim calmly fluttered down to the bank. Nicco was keeping a place for her. Thankfully, all of the other first were still in the Castle of Fire keeping watch over her other two charges. Luckily they hadn't wanted to come here to witness this show of power. Powers that she had no way to explain.

Softly she landed just an arm's length away from Nicco, who gave a slight bow yielding to her will. "People of the Mystic Woods stand aside and allow these Fey room."

The warriors did not yield, but those who were not trained guards nor fighters took to their misty forms. It was the most concession that she was going to receive until her guards were satisfied that none wished to harm her.

Yet none of the Fey spoke. Their eyes now locked on her. All looking apprehensive and fearful. Many still breathing heavily, not yet understanding what had just happened.

A New World

"I am the goddess Primitiva. I collected you from the Void cross me and your fate will be one worse than the dishonor you have already faced."

Her eyes shifted just slightly. Motion coming close to the river's bank. A man. A Feyen man bronze skin and midnight black hair was clearly shifting closer toward her. One of the royal Fey. If she was correct, he was from one of the dark stars. The home of Dark Fey. Those who were not easily controlled. Still, he was weak compared to her.

For the moment she pretended not to notice him drawing closer to her. "For the moment you will be given anything that you need. In time as you settle into your surroundings, I will help you find your place within my home. As this star offers many different climates and habitats I'm sure you will find places that best represent who you wish to be." She paused then choose to speak directly to those of royal blood. "Those of you that are of royal blood, you will be housed in my castle of night. You will be paired with those who I see fit not of your choosing."

The Fey, who had been slowly approaching suddenly stopped and hissed, "I have never heard of a goddess. And I will not blindly listen to… "

With nothing more than a look, she began pulling air from his lungs… Pulling his blue life blood to drip from his nose. Just a heartbeat or two from what would have killed him. She released his lungs and allowed him to gasp for air. "I can be merciful or not. The choice is up to you. If you live that will be up to me. Any questions?"

His body collapsed to the ground before his lungs filled with enough air to breath without gasping. Slowly he shook his head. "Now what is your name since you seem to be the one who is most vocal."

Still gasping for air, his dull smoky gray eyes looked up at her and for the first time noticed her wings. Not wings of a Fey… or at least not those of a known Fey.

But those of a creator. She had called herself goddess… oh, but she was so much more. He could see that now. He could see the mistake of speaking to her as he had. Swallowing hard, he closed his eyes, "Honua. I was once crown prince of Amaris. The largest dark star. I…" Again he swallowed, having never needed to explain his actions to anyone. "… I apologize for my actions I have never heard of one more powerful then Azia." Or at least none that were still alive.

Prim nodded once. "Nicco please have the carriages come to collect those whose blood runs blue. All others see they are taken to my meadows. There is plenty of food there for them. Once they are rested see that they are settling within the castle."

Nicco stepped closer, "Perhaps they all would like some coverings until proper ones can be made for them?"

"Very well. I must return to my private castle. I will not be disturbed."

A New World

Her private castle. The one that she had created for those who were no longer capable of life. The ones that were never truly dead. That is what she was telling him. With a tip of his head Nicco smiled, "Of course my queen. I can take care of everything here.: He paused relaying the orders to his people, then he gave her a small nod before saying, "The others can take care of the children until you return."

CHAPTER 16: GOVARD

A man stepped in front on him. His arm preventing him from moving forward. The look he cave this fey must have conveyed his questions well enough since he started to speak.

"Don't be a fool. There will be well enough time to speak to Prim. But not here. Not now."

"You know…" Fool obviously he knew her enough to casually call her Prim.

"Aye, I knew her but knew her her sister better." He paused and smiled, "I'm Zale. Crown prince… or would have been crown prince of Obsidian."

Obsidian. There wasn't a builder that didn't know the name . Their forges were legendary. Primitive but they produced no finer in blades. Or in fighters.

Reaching out his hand he tried to smile, "Govard, um..er… crown prince of Arcadian."

"The star that values tech over bronze."

At that he smiled, "Something like that." His eyes scanned the area, "I don't see Talos."

"Talos? He was with you when…"

A New World

"We jumped into the void together. He was… is… my eldest friend and makes a damn good guard." He paused, "When he's not scolding me for playing in forge and not mingling with the women."

A twinkle of mischief lit Zale's sea blue eyes. "Come on lets go talk to some one that might be in charge. Best if we figure out where we are… and get an audience with Prim. And pray that she doesn't kick my ass for being here and not protecting her sister."

He didn't know why but he liked this man. At least for the moment. Only time would tell if he truly was a friend or yet another to be kept close and guard against the blade pointed at his back.

There were too many people here to find any that looked in charge of anything. Fey from every type of star city that he knew of. Royal Fey, guards, all mixed with servants. Yet Zale didn't seem to me looking for anyone who was Fay. No he had headed off to the very first person that he could find that didn't have wings.

Zale had calmly approached the man with dark skin and pointed teeth. The man who just standing doing nothing looked more terrifying than any of the Fey that now were slowly moving about seeking others of their star.

"Hello, good sir?" Zale bobbled keeping his eyes on the man before him. "Would you point the way to whomever maybe in charge now that the … ur… um… goddess had left?"

The man didn't seem to move yet a breath more and another man materialized before them. Govard's only thought was Oh shit. "Zale?"

The man in the black suit narrowed his eyes. His face was narrow and handsome. The heat of seduction that swirled around him nearly intoxicating. There and gone as he relaxed, "I hear you needed to speak to someone in charge?"

Zale finally glanced over to Govard and smiled. Clearly not as confident in negotiation as he had thought. Forcing what he hoped was a friendly smile Govard croaked out, "My friend here is… was … a friend of Prim. And…"

"And we were hoping to speak to her?" Zale finished lamely.

The man looked both of them up and down. A darkness in his eyes that warned trouble, yet he didn't move for more than a few heart beats. "And your names? Perhaps that would be helpful in making the request."

Whatever stoic and frightening posture he has been trying to covey had melted enough to have warmth in the words. Not enough that the question wasn't any less a command. But it was along way from a barked order.

"I am Zale. Crown prince of Obsidian. This is my friend Govard. Crown prince of Arcadian."

The man tip his head in a slight show of respect. "Then you may address me as Nicco the king of the Estroe. These are my lands and my people.."

Oh shit. If this was the king, not some person that the woman had placed in charge… "I thought the…. goddess.. was in charge?"

Zale turned to him quickly. His hand connecting to the back of Govard's head. "My friend…"

The apology was cut short from Nicco coughing back a laugh. "No, no you're friend is fine. Come we'll get you registered in. Karnack will get you both sorted out. And I'll make the request of the goddess." He turned to leave, "It maybe some time before she is able to speak to you. She's not one to shun a request but it will be some time."

"Thank you you're…."

Govard stopped when Nicco turned to him the look warning him to silent himself.

"Lord Nicco. There is only one highness here and that is the goddess. She will tell you how to address her. But boys, take what you know and forget it. From what I know about your homeland the rules don't apply here."

One of the men… guards… that had been standing around watching the group had approached him and Zale not a moment after Nicco had left. It was a strange moment to see the man one moment walking into the wood and the next for him to become a cloud of black mist.

"Did he?" Govard had asked the guard. Who in turn just looked puzzled at the question. However, while leading them to this person who was called Karnack,finally answered.

"We are in the Mystic woods. Those who dwell here are first under the rule of Nicco but don't cross him. His temper is not one to be trifled with. "

A New World

"And the goddess?" Zale had hedged into the conversation.

"Prim is Prim. She is the ruler of all we have. From coast to coast. She create what we need and in turn we serve her will. None here will go against her. Except Trolls. They might but only to be saved from either the farms where they are food or the mines where they live freely."

It was clear after that any answer would only leave them more confused. After all what was a troll? And where had they came from?

The man stood aside when they entered an area with two long lines then a third much shorter one. "Nicco says you are royal fey, you belong to the shorter line."

Govard narrowed his eyes taking in what he saw. The two long line had to have nearly a thousand fey in each. Clothing from every star that he had ever hear of and at least two who hailed from Nexus.

"Zale?" he nodded at the two dark fey who looked more out of place,

"By the gods. What has Azia been doing since Despina tried to kill me?"

He didn't ask. Didn't want to know at least not yet about that remark. However he did say, "Apparently giving Prim an army."

"Come on we better get in the correct line before-"His words were cut off by a woman who yelled.

"Zale? I should kick your ass right here and now."

Zale turned snapping to attention trying to find the source of the voice before cursing under his breath. There not far away was a young woman dressed in what was common clothing of Nexus. A thread bare head scarf and matching dress only it covered a silvery dress made of midnight color. As she took her scarf from her face she truly looked ready to attack.

"Friend of yours?"

Zale crossed his arms. "Govard meet my sister. Crown Princess Kaida of Nexus. She is also my twin."

"How does that-"

"Long story. Perhaps we can get drunk enough to discuss it."

Govard watched her approached and knew the fluid movements of a huntress. Her every step deliberate. Her hand held loosely at her side. Before she got close enough to Zale , Govard step grabbing her wrist and pulling her ting to him.

Her sight shielded blade dropping to the floor before anyone noticed the scuffle.

A New World

Hissing Govard leaned close to her ear, "We can't afford fighting right now."

Her eyes blazed in anger as she jerked away. "I wouldn't have killed him. But he deserves a blade between the ribs for leaving to deal with everything."

Yes it going to be an interesting story. But not now.

"Fine, deal with it later right now lets do this and figure out where we are."

For only a dozen fay the line seems to move slowly. Too slowly. Yet stepping up to the table Govard saw why. The man, possibly some fay without wings looked more like a benign clerk in a shop. One that had been spared death just to keep track of numbers and scrolls.

Oh he looked young enough but like all fey looks could be very deceitful.

The man glance up over half moon glasses. And waited for a breath. "Ah so the crown prince of Arcadian has ventured to me at last."

It made it sound like he had been waiting for him , and he the crown prince knew better than to keep any elder waiting. "I was delayed?"

"No matter, we'll get you settled into the castle of Night shortly. Then figure out who is needed where." The man paused dipping his quill in the ink well. "I am Karnack. Nicco has taken special interest in you and your friend." he said while putting a few words on paper.

"Is that a good thing?"

Karnack let out a quick laugh. Slowly he stood, "Come you and your friend , Zale is it? Should come with me. The others seem to be all muscle and no brains. Donny can take care of them if Prim doesn't."

He fell into step Karnack noticing the fine robes. Something a royal might wear. "Are of you a king of something as well?"

Stopping suddenly Karnack looked at him with the most puzzling look, "Of those who rule there is the goddess who rules all. Nicco who rules the Estroe. Ean who rules the Draken, and Donovan who rules all with wings. Alec and myself claim only the title of Lord as the goddess demands we hold a title." He patted Govard on the back. "You will be sorted out soon enough."He looked ahead, "And see you're friend is here now. And who is the young lady."

A New World

Zale took a deep breath pulling his sister to his side. "This is my sister Kaida. I hope her sharp tongue and even sharper blades won't be too much of an issue."

"Bah! She can not harm any unless the goddess so wills it. Now come the carriage is that way. We will be at the castle of Night before the the sun fully sets."

Chapter 17: Zale

Rubbing his hands over his face, Zale closed the bedchamber door behind him. The ride was not as long as he had thought it might have been, but keeping Kaida from doing anything rash… now that had been exhausting. Well that had been until the carriage spouted wings and started to fly.

Yes then his nearly unshakable sister had sat still clinging to him. Well at least once in their life he could say he found something to actually scared her shitless.

But now that that was over he was going to take some time for himself and…

Bang.

Bang.Bang. Bang.

He turned quickly to open the door before the damn thing was made into splinters. 'What…" He swallowed whatever else he was going to say as he was looking at an angered dark fey. "Can I help you?"

The man brushed him aside and entered without being invited. Not that he was going to say anything. Not one word when surviving a dark fey it was always better to yield.

A New World

"Karnack said your sister needed some one to settle her down."

That was putting it mildly. "She's not in here."

A blaze of dark fury lit his eyes as his voice lowered, "I see that. But where did the little assassin slip away to?"

Well shit if this fey knew what his sister was other than a royal fey… "What makes you think…" another word that wasn't helpful would have gotten him killed. Seeing the rage in the man building. Oh, he knew the only way to live now was to answer correctly, "… She likes quiet places. Areas that she can practice her skills without actually killing anyone."

The dark fay nodded once, "That which guards the castle will find her. They won't kill her this time. But this is a warning, I will not tolerate disobedience in the goddess' absence."

"I understand and am thankful for the warning." Zale moved slightly away from the door to allow for the man to leave easily. "May I know your name so if I see her…"

"Donovan. Lord Donovan." he took a few steps closer to Zale. "I tolerate children acting like little beast. But I will not put up with youths as old as you doing the same."

"Donovan! That is enough."

The evil hiss that came from the doorway was enough for the dark fay to take a step back. His eyes looking around the room trying to find what didn't belong. Then backed up more as Nicco took a step from around the doorway. Picking his teeth with a bone of something. "Nicco?"

A cautious tone from a dark fey warned of two things. First off whomever held the man's loyalty would not allow his temper to be continue. That was common within the stars. The other possibility is the slender man with the sharp pointed teeth was more volatile than the dark fay.

To Zale's knowledge there was nothing deadlier than a dark fey. Yet looking between the two he could no longer bet on that.

A flick of the wrist and the sliver of bone vanished, "The girl belongs to the goddess. She will over see her training personally."

Donovan looked puzzled as he asked, "She knows…"

"The goddess has returned moments ago. You are to see to the children coming morning. She has taken special interest in this one." Nicco paused and his smile was more chilling than reassuring, "She is ready to see you now."

A New World

The castle was eerie and dark. Even for a castle that housed dark fey this one seemed off somehow. Colder. More distant. Darker.

"Does Prim spend a lot of time here?" he asked to the man walking next to him. The king of the Estroe.

Nicco paused then shrugged, "It depends on where Alec wants to be. He likes it here. And Prim built this for him."

He nearly stumbled over his feet. "Prim? She build this for…"

"You haven't met Alec yet. But when you see them together you'll understand." Grabbing Zale's arms , Nicco pulled him to a stop, "We all would appreciate if you don't tell the fool what is right before his eyes. Prim's counsel take great joy in watching how jealous he becomes."

"And no one is in fear of what might happen if…"

"Nah, Alex and I fight. Depending on Prim's mood she may find it entertaining or not. But he holds her heart.

I hold her ears and eyes. There is nothing I don't see or hear."

And there was the warning. This king was more than a friend to Prim. He was her second in command. Not so different from some of the other cities. His father had his wife. A wife that he, the crown prince called mother. She had raised him. But his father's second in command was the Queen of Nexus. She was the eyes and ears for so many. And none crossed her.

"I understand. Don't cause trouble unless I want to deal with you."

"Something like that." As Nicco started walking again he shoved his hand into his pockets. "As in all places there are factions. There are those loyal to Prim and will do anything to protect her."

"And those who seek to destroy her even if it means destroying themselves?"

"Aye. But watch who you trust young prince of Obsidian. You may wish to live long enough to return home."

It was a warning. Maybe even a forewarning. Either way it was one he would not ask to be clarified.

A New World

Chapter 18: Nicco

He didn't want to disturb her while she was here. Not while she was dealing with whatever memories that she was hiding from. Memories that she trying to escape. Yet, he was the only one privileged enough to call upon her.

Still it made this no less easier.

A deep breath and took in the the rare and terrifying beauty of the castle of bones. Some were as old as this star. Some, those had been creations that the goddess had created. But the rest.

Ah, well only he and the goddess knew the bones were still living beings. Ones that no living thing could kill. Nor could even kill the first king of the Eostre.

But those were thoughts for another day.

Right now he needed to speak to her and find out about the young boy. All of the fey really, but he would start with the young ones.

A New World

The throne room door was open. The sentries gone for the moment. Not that they were needed, but the goddess like the idea that they were there. Trusted members of her court sworn to protect her.

Quit silly really when she could kill anything she wished, anytime she wished.

But the sentries being gone meant she was expecting him. And if she was expecting him then he had already kept her waiting long enough.

Two steps within the room and he knelt down. His eyes lowered to the floor waiting to be noticed. He would stay here all night if she required it. Thou she never did.

"Rise Nicco, you are a king and kneel before no one." Her breezy voice washed over him easing a bit of tension he had been holding.

Getting to his feet he asked, "How is the boy?"

"He will be resting till morning. What was done …" Fire blazed in her eyes before she blinked it away, "I'll deal with later." She paused getting settled on her throne of bones and flesh. "You did not come here to speak of the child."

"One of the fey asked to speak to you."

"Which fey. Few knew of me when I resided in my home star."

"He claims his name is Zale? I believe he hailed from Obsidian."

"Zale?' she whispered. "Zale is here? Is my sister. Starlis. Is she here as well?"

She looked excited. Panicked. A bit concerned. And then there was another thing that he couldn't name. "No, Queen Starlis wasn't present on this particular day."

She sagged back against the throne. "I know not to be relived or frightened. Yet…" She got to her feet, "I will meet him at once."

"And the boy?"

"I will return after speaking to Zale." A smile twitched her lips, "Azia made a mistake killing so many royal children."

"How convenient he gave you a stronger army should he come here."

A New World

She padded over to him. A twinkle of mischief in her eyes. "I already have an army Nicco. What he gave me was the armies of the stars."

The gate of the dead had brought them directly to the throne room of Darke. The castle of Night already quite when everyone had just been brought here not hours before.

Narrowing his eyes he listened not the goddess who was settling in on her dark throne. Not to the birds cooing just beyond the window. But rather to the on goings of the castle.

He had asked the shadows to stay with the royal fey. Just a precaution really. If needed none would be able to leave their chambers until summoned. Yet..

His head tilted to the side as he focused trying to understand what he was hearing.

"Nicco?" Prim's voice not worried but still questioning. She wouldn't demand he tell her what he knew, just trusted him to tell what she needed to know.

"One of the royals is a trained assassin. She had vanished from her chamber." He narrowed his eyes and turned to his queen. "The shadows are distress as they can't locate her. Donny, is searching." He paused, "Why would Donny search for her and who would have told him to?"

She let out a laugh. "Are you more concerned that he is searching for one little assassin or that your shadows can not find her?"

Ah bloody hell when said like that…

"She's in the under rooms playing with your poisons." He paused letting his queen decide if she was amused or angry. Since he saw laughter in her eyes he added, "Should I bring her here or have Zale brought first?"

"I will speak to Zale first. Should you find Donny please convey I will oversee the girl and her training. Perhaps, she can train me in what she knows as well."

That was scary thought and not one he would ever put to words. "Of course."

Nicco bowed polity then formed into dark mist. Few would see him coming this way, but the information he could gather in these moments would be needed. Yes needed so he knew what poisons the girl was dabbing with and what he would need to correct.

CHAPTER 19: ZALE

The door to the throne room was open. So different from that of Obsidian. Is father liked it closed to keep those who were beneath him from entering. Yet, it suited Prim. Or at least suited what he remembered of her.

Entering he didn't know if he should bow or not. Really wasn't sure on how to address her since Nicco was so informal. "Prim?" he asked hoping he would be permitted to speak to her as a lost friend.

"Come Zale sit with me." As she turned her hand over a seat next to her throne appeared. "There is much to discuss and you seem to be at the very center of most of it."

A he drew closer he smiled, "Starlis said you were the greatest seer that the star ever had."

"Yes, well she might have been bias being my sister."

He liked the sound of her voice. Breezy and relaxed. Not at all the harsh snobbish one he remember. Yet he laughed, "You could be right, but I still trust what she said."

A New World

She leaned back in her chair, "I did not see your death when I decided to leave the city. What I saw was you and her raising Avyanna."

"Yes well, the queen had other plans. Or so it appears."

For several moments neither spoke. Neither knew what to say or what to ask. Finally Prim asked, "Tell me about your sister?"

"I would rather tell you why my twin is the crown princess of Nexus."

She nodded one, "Fine start there."

"Some time ago, the former king decided to retire. Yet he had no heir of his own. Or at least no Male heir. Which made the world of difference in the eyes of the people. So he made his daughter choose a royal to rule with her as his queen. Publicly the crown would be ruled by the king. Privately…"

"By her."

"Hmm. And that suited her and the royal she choose just fine. He would have been sent to a catacombs and never would have ruled. Yet after the union, he met the Queen of Nexus."

Prim leaned in, "She is a very gifted seer from what is told."

"So she is. But it has always been speculation if she saw what she said or was just a way to bed my father. In either case she gave birth to Kaida and myself."

"Then you were raised on obsidian as the crown prince, and she on Nexus. I see how that would benefit both cities."

Now Zale leaned in, "Kaida spent half of each light cycle in each city. Or that is what was said. What wasn't said was that Nexus has been training her as an assassin since birth. Shivani also recently, or at least as recent as when I left to live with Starlis, had another child."

She leaned back on her throne and closed her eyes. "So what I have here is the crown Prince of Obsidian who has no blood ties to the star. The crown princess of Nexus who was never meant to rule anything. Whom is already skilled in blade and death. Obsidian looking at my sister for the cause of your death. And Nexus who will align with those they see fit." She paused, "Is that about right?"

Zale ran his fingers thru his hair , "That and according to lore both Obsidian and Nexus hold weapons that only the true ruler can wield."

Getting to her feet Prim paced the confines of the room. Her eyes looking to her narrow fingers yet what she was seeing was hard to tell. Abruptly she stopped. "Nicco?"

He glided into the room yet he hadn't been standing outside the doorway. Zale was certain of that.

A New World

Prim squared her shoulders then looked between him and Nicco. "What is said now will not be repeated. Do I have your word?"

Both men nodded.

War was coming. Still yet on the horizon, but was coming.

Prim had just confirmed that. From the embers in her fire red hair to the flames held within her wings. She knew, as did any living seer.

Zale laid back on his bed. They had time to build a life here. To train. To live. Really live as all fey should. But war was coming and the choices he made now would decide if he lived to see Obsidian once more or dye on the star so far away from the pull of Pallas.

CHAPTER 20: PRIMITIVA

She waited until one of the guards escorted Zale from the room. Waited long enough for the tall decorative doors to close. Waited long enough to turn the wood to stone before exploding into her rage.

The coverings of the windows burst into flames. Wood to ash. And some where the gargoyles screamed in warning. The goddess was enraged. Nicco was with her. Was the message that was carried. But only a few would hear those words and they would answer the call.

She fluttered around the room. Nicco always within her sites. He wasn't afraid of her. Wasn't fearful that she would strike him in anger. No he wasn't watching her, he was gathering ever ounce of information that he could before the first gathered.

Which they did not a moment later.

Alec was the first to enter looking ready for battle if that was what it took. Donovan was not far behind him with both Ean and Karnack following closely. One glance at Nicco and no one moved nor spoke.

"I should kill Azia here and now." Prim hissed out. "Take Shesha and destroy the entire city before his corruption spreads too far."

A New World

Nicco pushed away from the wall, "And should you succeed what would be the price? What lives would be changed?"

He would be the only one who would dare challenge her. But he was the only one that knew all of her secrets. All of them.

She finally settled on her throne with her dragon wings pulled tightly to her side. "It's a price too steep to pay."

Locking eyes with her Nicco let a smile twitch his blood red lips, "Then what is the queens command?"

He would travel to Pallas if she sent him. The destruction left in his wake …. the blood that would be spilled would be horrendous. More so after he got to taste true Fey blood.

"No, what I see needs to pass."

Seeing her calm Alec approached, "Then what do we need to prepare?"

"Lord Donovan you will train all of those who were at the mystic woods today. Test their abilities. Unlock those that are hidden. The children. I want all the children raised as those on the star have been."

Karnack nodded. "I'll see they are all placed in schools come morning. Their education will be the best that we can provide."

"As they grow I will find matches for the royal fey. Zale is matched with my sister should she survive. The young one, Magmas, he will wed Kaida. His power will be strong enough to withstand hers. And outside of him,Nicco is only one who would survive her."

With a nod Karnack smiled, "I will record that as soon I return to my study."

Donovan cracked his knuckles as he flexed, "And about the other one. The friend of this Zale?"

For a long time she sat there listening to her inner voice. Listening to the whispers that she tried to silence. "Nothing will ever be recorded of this day, aside of the marriages. The children of Orisus, Zale, Kaida, and Govard are to be trained with the expectation they will lead my armies. Donovan you are in charge of those arrangements."

"I request Daegal help with that training."

Daegal one of her trusted few. He had help with the troll rebellion some time ago and worked well among her first. Cunning and ruthless, yet he took orders as well as he gave them. "Agreed." she paused getting to her feet. "Is there anything else to be said?"

A New World

CHAPTER 11: FLINT

The feeling of floating brought him back to his body.

Something warm and soft covered him. His pain no longer filling every thought. The feeling of fingers passing through his hair.

Slowly his amber colored eyes fluttered opened. Even slower his vision cleared the haze of sleep as a shape took form before him. At first, it had been mist. Then fire. The flames, hot enough to give his body the warmth that he craved. Finally, a figure. A woman.

Radiant fire red hair that the volcanoes of Osiris could not do justice to. Then those eyes… those galaxy blue eyes complete with the stars… together with her narrow face "Your breathtaking." The words slipped out before he thought about saying them.

When she did not speak, he wondered if he had actually said them. After all, his mouth felt fuzzy numb as his tongue licked his dry lips. Hoarsely he asked, "Is this what death feels like?"

Slowly a shy smile formed on the woman's lips. "Hardly. But you, Flint, are not dead." Then her eyes lit up with amusement, "But you are trouble. Mostly forgiven since Magmas is also a known flirt."

A New World

He blinked unsure how this creature knew his name. Struggling to sit up, he took in more of her beauty. A thin frame and dragon wings. Wings of a creator. Her legs blending into a scaly tail. Long and coiled around her. Fins of golden fire at the end. A blink and the tail turned into legs. Whiffs of red mist creating a covering.

Asking "What are you?" would be rude so he asked instead, "You know my sire?"

She leaned forward in her seat. "I do. Though I think my first impression of him may have been wrong." Taking a measured breath, the woman added, "I am the queen Primitiva. You may call me Prim."

Carefully he tried to sit and found his body felt more like the lava in a bath then of a body, "I don't feel well."

"No, dear, I suppose you do not. Perhaps we should start with a simple conversation before we get better acquainted."

"Yes, I suppose that would be good."

Flint swallowed hard now seeing the room that he was held in. Bones for walls. Light illuminating out of nowhere. Red blood… a river on the floor. "This place… What is it?"

"This is my private castle. Those who are no longer capable of life dwell here. Their power feeds this place. At least until their bones turn to dust."

Alarmed, he pressed himself to the head of the bed. "You said I was not dead."

"Darling, I was asked to take you someplace safe. I cannot think of a safer place than among the greatest of my creations. For every bone that you see… it is that of a gifted warrior. Their blood is the river that you see. They are dormant now, but are still capable of being should I need them." She paused for just a heartbeat, "Do you doubt what I tell you?"

Flint shook his head. His father had taught him that a creator was to be treated with the greatest respect. Never doubt them.

Never ask them to prove their power. A single creator was a hundred times more dangerous than all other Fey combined. Their power… their gifts alone could do so many great things. Or so many horrible deeds. It made sense now. His father had been preparing him for this. "What will become of me?"

Prim slowly got to her feet. Feet that never touched the ground. Her hand passing lovingly over the bones that she passed. Then she turned, her wings no longer visible. The mist that had covered her turning into a shimmering midnight blue dress. Her fire red hair cascading down her back. A simple crown of silver now adorned on her head. "That is up to you. You may come and live among my creations and be with your brothers. Or you may stay here until you are ready. It makes little difference to me."

A New World

Before he could think, Flint squeaked out, "My brothers are alive?"

"Alive, yes, but not how you remember them. All enchantments that made them appear older and stronger are now gone. As they are with you. Those who come here cannot hide behind enchantments such as those."

Again, he swallowed and held his hands out before him. Small hands. A child's hands. Then at his sides… stone gray wings. His wings, they had been reformed. Carefully, he pulled them around himself. "My brother's, they have their wings?"

"They do. As do all those who have them naturally." Swinging his legs over the side of the bed he gulped.

There were several feet between the floor and the bed. A river of blood waiting to catch him. It hadn't been until then that he realized what he had been seeing. She was walking… hovering well above the ground. The floor that had looked within reach was in fact too far away. She was creating an illusion to keep him at ease. An illusion that he broke just by sitting up. There was no wall of bones… there were mountains of bones. Some still covered in flesh. There, just at the edge of his vision he could just make out shapes.

Focusing on them, he could see… could make out… bodies bathing in the river. Gulping air, he tried to smile, "I would like to be with my brothers. If you would permit me."

Slowly Prim drew closer once again. "You are better mannered than your brothers. I should hope you teach them all that you know."

A New World

CHAPTER XX: ALEC & NICCO

"What in the name of all I have created do the two of you think you were doing!" Primitiva yelled her voice shaking loose several bones of long forgotten citizens. The echoes rolling over the vast empty landscape like deep thunder.

Both of her favorites flinched. Over the centuries they have butted heads a time or two never had they done anything to make her this mad… mad enough to make her bring them to her under kingdom where the dead still roamed. The place where her temper could run without recourse.

Carefully Nicco swallowed, "I was only trying to make the children relax. I meant no harm goddess."

For just a moment she let a vine of dark mist wrapping around Nicco's throat prohibiting his transformation or escape. "I should strip you of your gifts right now. Leave you for my children to feast on. I should…"

A New World

Alex shifted his weight deliberately shifting her attention to him, "The fault is mine goddess. I have been too occupied with the fallen Fey and misinterpreted Nicco's intention."

She let Nicco go seeing the fear in his eyes. A long, tense moment longer so that he could understand the rage that was deep within her eyes and she pointed a long, narrow finger at both of them, "This will not happen again. Is that understood?"

"Yes, goddess." Hanging their heads like two boys who had been scolded without understanding why, both Alec and Nicco said in unison.

Sharply she turned from both of them, then hissed. "You both will remain here until I decide what I will do. For this one time, you are saved from my pets." A clap of thunder louder than any storm then the doorway appeared. "You should come to the understanding right now… this silly game you play with each other ends… now. I will not tolerate this game any longer…"

As she stepped through the doorway they both breathed in relief. "Shit."

Nicco rubbed his throat, feeling the bruise already forming.

The first bruise since he could remember. "She is more irritated than I have ever seen."

"Irritated? Irritated? Damn it Nicco don't you realize you could of cost us our lives with that damn stunt. She's not Irritated… she's pissed off and overwhelmed. "

Kicking the dirt that seemed to cover everything Nicco shook his head, "No something else is wrong far beyond us. And it started with the boys coming here."

"At least that we can agree on." Alec paused, seeing something moving far beyond the edge of his vision. "What pets does she house here?"

"You would know better than I but I think those here do not need food or air to survive."

Giving his brother, a menacing look Alec growled with frustration, "How delightful. More so now that I am stuck here with you along with them."

Turning Nicco shrugged, "Well, I'm going to find the castle it may yield some answer to help the goddess. You can do as you please."

Alec turned, "If I could kill you I would… but you may have a point this time."

"I always have a point to everything that I do. It is you that have yet to understand that."

Taking a step over a pile of fresh bones Alec hissed, "Then please enlighten me."

A New World

"You see the goddess and I enter her private room… You see that the room is sealed from all others. You assume what we

do is what you do with her. Yet you do not look beneath the surface. In all of the years, you have not considered why Ean and I go into that room."

For a long time, Alex didn't speak instead choose to watch where he stepped carefully not to step on the bones of Prim's chosen. Letting Nicco's words tumble in his head, he finally hissed, "So what do you and Ean do with her?"

Nicco let out a soft laugh, "You make a poor excuse for a guard. But since you asked, we keep her informed on several things. Only Eostre can be everywhere at once. Our ability to travel… to see and hear all that is around us. Couple that with my ability as the king of my people I can see and hear all that they do. Or at least most of the time. It is very confusing to hear thousands of conversations at one time, but it is useful."

Alec paused too stunned for words. "You have never mentioned that once. Damn you, do you realize how many times that could have become useful over the centuries?"

Nicco shrugged, "I am not a guard. It is not up to me to keep our lands safe. That is what you are to be doing. However, considering the amount of true Fey that is now in our lands it is becoming more apparent for me to help you."

He could strangle Nicco. And would if the demon would stand still long enough without turning into mist. "You are infuriating."

Rolling his eyes Nicco pointed. "I think that is the castle."

All of the castles that they knew were built up into towering structures. This one was round and made of more bones. "Am I to believe that every living person who becomes no longer living is brought here?"

"That or the bones that are too hard for even me to eat. Prim said once that every tissue carries the power of the one who body it once came from. From her point of view bones are tissue."

"How wonderful. Remind me if I die I do not want to become a wall."

Nicco bared his teeth in an insincere smile as he joked, "Of course not. You could become a chair."Alec narrowed his eyes and hissed, "I hate you."

It wasn't a castle, but a maze filled with rooms. Doors made of pulled flesh. Behind the doors were those who should no longer be alive. Trolls who had died from some illness. Ill-tempered and trapped behind the doors. Their drool still dripping from their jaws. Another room. A creature with large coral red eyes and a breathtakingly lovely face.

Until gills came from behind her ears, hiding her hair. Her legs turning into a tail and her arms into fire. Too quickly Nicco closed the door before she could attack. "What was that?"

"You sound scared for an almighty king."

"Shut up Alec." Nicco paused. "Perhaps we should not have come here."

Seeing the great and fearless king becoming unnerved Alex gave a conspiring smile as he said, "Perhaps what we seek is deep inside.

Chapter 3: Starlis

With the tribute coach landing safely on the platform of her own Star City Starlis shivered. First, she would do what needed to be done with the hateful little demon spawn that was Griffith.

Hopefully, he liked nectar. Then again, she didn't know a Fey that could refuse it either.

Letting the messenger open the door for her, Starlis took a single step her eyes scanning the once filled streets. Just years ago, when she was yet a small child she played happily on these streets. Fathers taught their sons warcraft. She remembered watching them teach the boys to do battle with dull blades. Mothers sang as they created glorious works of art. As they made meals for their families.

Long gone were those days. Now adult men were either guard for the crowns pleasure or slaves. Either way, their abilities were no longer theirs. Their children were taken from their arms the moment the child could feed and bathe themselves. Mothers no longer sang with joy, they were now forced into silence. Their powers now seeping away every day into the very star that they lived.

If Primitiva was right, she, the queen of Lunaista, could stop this madness and return her home back to its former glory. She had the power to end this. She had to end this. No, she would end this.

She could no longer afford not to.

As she made her way to the palace, she heard the snap of another whip as it hit flesh. She heard the wails of a mother as her child was torn from her arms. The screams of a child having their wings ripped from their backs.

Her feet moved with earnest now. This ended now.

As she entered the heart of her castle she checked her stride. She needed to play the part of the subdued queen. She needed to appear indifferent. No matter what was on the other side of the now cloudy crystal door… she had to see this through.

Opening the door just enough to slip into the room unnoticed she breathed out a sigh of relief. Griffith was meagerly sitting at a long table enjoying a meal. "More nectar your grace?"

His blue-gray eyes studied her as he swallowed, "You have been gone a while."

"Only to visit some of the other queens. My pets bore me."

A cruel smile formed on his tiny lips. "Perhaps it's time for another one to take their place on this pitiful star. I will request one from the shadow stars. It will be a pleasure to tame one."

Creeping over to the table she poured the pale-yellow liquid into his glass. "I was told this is the best nectar within the stars.

Your father's favorite vintage, I believe."

Eagerly Griffith snatched the glass. "It's about time you did something to please me." Then he drank every drop from the glass. "Pity there isn't more." He slammed the glass down shattering it on the table.

Starlis watched as a maid hurried over to clean up the broken pieces apologizing for the glass being inadequate.

Rolling his eyes Griffith pushed away from the table. "I am going for a walk. Do not follow me."

Lowering her gaze Starlis mumbled, "Of course your grace." Then she moved to the side allowing him to pass freely.

A New World

It wasn't until a guard rushed in that Starlis began to worry. "What is it?" She forced herself to snap out.

"He… The royal… The Azia his son… he just…."

Blubbering fool. What was so horrid that the man couldn't string together a few words to form a coherent thought. Then she heard it. Jumping up from her seat she gasped, "He just what?"

The guard steadied himself preparing to be killed just for delivering the news. "He jumped into the Void."

By the gods, what did she just do? No, she had done nothing wrong. She only gave the boy some nectar. What she had left would be tested by the Azia. Looking unconcerned she turned back to her crystal throne. It wasn't until she fussily took a seat that she even tried to speak. "Please inform the Azia that his son pulled such a distasteful act. I'm sure he will want a full account of what happened here today."

The guard paled until his once golden skin was the color of ash. He nodded only once as he turned to leave.

Starlis didn't need to wait long for the arrival of Azia. Actually, had to wait for a far less time than she would have ever thought. As he came to the double doors he used a gust of wind to blow them open not caring if they shattered or not. Unfazed by his temper she slowly stood, "Azia."

His eyes blazed with anger, "What did you give to my boy!"

Holding the small jar up she showed him the liquid that still resided. "Only nectar my lord. Would you like to test it?"

With long strides, he approached her snatching the jar from her hands. With nothing more than his thumb, he broke open the cap. Slowly he sniffed the contents. Sweet and spicy. Taking a single drop, it rolled on his tongue. Golden honey. Nothing about the beverage said it was tainted. And every spell that he cast all came back only that it was nectar.

Throwing the jar across the room Azia hissed as the glass shattered as it crashed against the solid crystal wall, "What did you do to make him jump?"

"I do not know what you are implying my lord. We discussed my boredom with my pets, which prompted me to visit a few of other Star Cities. Which you gave me permission to do seeing he was here to oversee this Star City in my absence. Once I returned I refilled his glass." She paused seeing the hate still seething in his eyes. "I don't know what caused him but he had threatened to jump several times before. He was one for theatrics always trying things just to see if he lived."

A New World

Azia's eyes blazed with anger as his voice lowered into a deep growl, "Are you saying my son was unstable?"

"Of course, not my lord. But the offspring from two different kinds of Fey sometimes does wield unfavorable result." Or very freighting ones like those of her sister. But this was not something that she would say. Least of all to him.

Sagging in her seat Starlis closed her eyes. Challenge one complete. Now she had a day to figure out the rest. The Azia would never believe that another royal child jumped into the Void. At least not one from this star. Not now when he was receiving reports of the other royal star children being claimed as unfit and tossed into the Void by the rulers of their own Star Cities. Not when several of the adults on those stars were also being forced into the Void. All of their power now forever lost.

Getting to her feet she shuffled to the door of the throne room. Passing a maid, she held her head high and growled, "I want every wall, window, and everything that should be see through to be scrubbed. I grow tired at this filth. And make it known I require this of every resident as well."

She hurried past making her way to the inner sanctum. Just outside the only solid door of her little star, she spotted a guard.

The way he was trying to avoid her wasn't uncommon. "You, come here."

"My queen?" His voice as soft as a whisper. Too much fear from speculation about what she would require from him.

"Stand guard here. I do not wish to be disturbed." Relief too apparent in his eyes as he nodded.

Once inside she sighed. How would she ever get through all of these scrolls before Avyanna returned? How to find the law that her sister hinted about among all these stacks of rolled parchment. This was hopeless. Reaching for one that looked aged she sagged against the wall. This was hopeless she was never going to find whatever she needed to.

She was never going to get through all of these scrolls.

Never going to find the answer.

No, she had to find … what… her eyes scanned an ancient scroll. The trial of the royals. "What do I have here?" And why hadn't I heard about this before? She wondered.

A New World

Her eyes read through the text. Carefully word for word. How did Primitiva know about this text? No better yet… would Azia allow this to happen?

Yes… an amazing smile formed on her lips. He would have to. This law… this trial was set by the Silent Ones themselves.

Licking her lips, she stopped herself from laughing. Either her darling niece was going to come face to face with her mother or… may the gods take mercy on her… she would come face to face with the Silent Ones. Either way, this was the answer that she had been looking for.

Going to her private room she felt as light as a feather. Filled with more joy than she had in forever long. She needed to look like the queen of Lunaista. She needed to be the Fey her sister thought that she could be. She needed to be cruel and cunning. She needed to sound like a royal Fey not some spineless house Fey.

Drawing a bath, she soaked away all her doubts. All of her fears. Washed away the dull grime that has built up in her hair for far too long. Scrubbed her skin until she could see the tiny specks of gold once again shining just beneath her skin.

With the last drop of water leaving her bath she let her old self leave with it. Gone was the girl who saw only the best. Gone was the Queen who allowed herself to be ruled over. Gone was the fail ruler of Lunaista. Today she would greet her niece as she should have all those years ago.

Today she would be the queen and absolute ruler of this star.

She answered to know one. Today she would take her little city back.

Pulling a silver dress from its hanger she narrowed her eyes.

Her mother had never dressed to intimidate. No, she had done so during her Culling. She understood that now. As she also understood the cruelty that she forced upon her pets. She did so to save the others … to save the citizens.

Well, she was not her mother. And she would not permit harm to any who she ruled over. That to stopped today. That stopped as soon as Avyanna left for the trials.

Her dress was shimmering silver covering her chest leaving her flat belly exposed. Two strands of material attached the top to her skirt at the sides. The skirt cut short in the front then ended at her feet in the back. Stepping in front of her mirrored glass Starlis smiled. Her gold hair like a waterfall of sunlit gold cascading down her back. Her crown silver and shining. She was ready.

The sound of breathing from her door had her facing away from her mirror to her husband. "Why do you look at me that way?"

Slowly he pushed off the door. He had never spoke since the trials. Didn't even remember his name after all of this time. Still, he could not help but to smile. "I have never seen you look lovelier."

She turned back to the mirror, "I'm not trying to look lovely. I am trying to look like a queen."

Coming up behind her, he kissed her neck and whispered, "Then you have succeeded." His lips hovered over her collarbone savoring this single moment with her. "Avyanna will arrive shortly."

Keeping his arm around her, she turned, "You have never come to me like this."

"You made it clear the night we were joined you already had an heir. And taking a mate was for appearances. With Avyanna ascending soon I thought a single moment …" He let the rest trail off no longer able to keep her gaze.

Placing her hand on his handsome chiseled face she sighed, "I want you to do something and not ask questions."

"You command is absolute my queen."

Swallowing hard she made her choice. "Find all those on this star with royal blood. I am banishing you all to the Void."

Horror fell on his face, as did the fear. "Am I not worthy to feed the catacombs?"

"You and all those with royal blood are more than worthy. That is why you must feed the Void. I cannot explain further but I will not allow another moment of pain to come to you. Now go. You must be gone the moment Avyanna comes to the palace."

He blinked away his doubts. "You will no longer have a guard left in the palace."

"I know. One will not be needed. Now go."

A New World

Chapter 4: Govard

Bang!

The sound of the door woke him fro his sleep. His eyes were open yet the room was dark. Too dark to see just a few inches from his face. Pulling the cover back around his shoulder, he gave himself a heartbeat before flicking a thought at the hearth to light the fire.

A breath more and started to sit up.

Bang! The sound louder this time which made his wonder what was making the door remain closed.

"Alight, I'm up." He said he stumbled from the bed. As he reached the door he mumbled, "Can it get any colder here?"

Before he could reach the door a hand grabbed his shoulder. After being her a day Govard knew only one person who would come in this quietly and grab him from behind. Calmly he said, "Lord Nicco? Can I help you with something?"

The breath was warm on his neck. Yet it still sent a chill. "Don't answer the door."

That quiet warning. The warm breath. And he slowly removed his hand from the handle. "Who…"

"Not who. What. One of Alec's pets escaped. No one else seemed bothered that someone was knocking. Nor cared."

"Most of the other cities don't bother knocking." The snort of a laugh was enough to ease the tension he had been feeling since Nicco grabbed him. Yet the King of Estroe hadn't released him yet either. "Something else?"

Slowly Nicco flexed his fingers into Govard's shoulder. A move that most of even the most skilled warrior would tense at. Yet, "I don't frighten you do I?"

"To fear someone because they are different is foolish. As of yet you have done nothing that I've witness that would cause fear." But what he had heard it wasn't smart to ignore the threat either.

The fingers that held the shoulder relaxed. "I can see why Prim has taken an interest in you." Nicco paused and was silent for more than a normal breath. "The beast is back in it's nest. Word of caution unless you know what is knocking at this time of night, it's best not to bother it."

Turning to face the man Govard tried not to smile. Tried even harder not to sound disrespectful, "And how exactly should I know who is on the other side of a closed door?"

The smile was bone chilling, yet seemed more of a true smile than one that meant harm, "Try asking who is there." Then Nicco took a step back looking Govard over, "Know this only those you who you allow access to this room can enter. Except those Prim has granted access. The corridors … eh …. just don't wonder too far in the dark."

"I take it there are things more dangerous than you lurking the halls?"

"There are none more dangerous than my kind. But things, creatures, that are just as deadly." Nicco locked eyes with him until he got the nod that he understood the warning. "Now, get some rest. Prim wants to speak with you after first light."

"Is this request being made of others?" It was a general question so why did Nicco look puzzled.

"There is only one here of your kind Prince Govard. And the goddess has need of your talents."

The sun was not yet over the horizon. Not even yet kissing the night sky. Yet there was enough light to call it first light. Or that was what Govard reasoned with himself when something cold and wet touched his skin and the he woke with a loud thud on an even colder and harder floor.

Getting his eyes fully open and rubbing his back side from the fall, he tried to get to his feet. The hand that grabbed him had him instead kneeling.

Looking to his right he saw the dark fey kneeling beside him. "Lord…'

"Shhhhh. The goddess is in a mood. Whatever is done make sure you do it according to whatever up bringing that you know."

Ah, bloody hell. Prim as queen those trusted were relaxed around. Feared only when fear was warranted. For this fey to call her the goddess. Whatever was happening was not any version of normal. And was warranted with something more than just fear.

Several breaths and the room warmed. The dark title floor crackled as veins of red formed. Gray smoke edged the embers of the veins. To watch it was memorizing. To have stone that changed …

Until the heat of the stone became too hot.Too burning. Sweat dripped from his face. The a voice cold and dark came from behind them. "That worthless fool. Can he not see he will destroy everything that keeps the silent ones held within their home? Kill the strong to leave the weak to defend against what? There is not any born that can withstand what he is creating." Fire blazed up from the titles just for a breath. "Damn him."

With a cough Nicco's voice stopped the rant of the goddess. "My queen? You're guest as requested. Perhaps, after we can find a solution to the noxious problem?"

If she responded Govard didn't hear. But the room cooled to a reasonable temperature. "Rise, I won't have a conversation to those kneeling."

Getting to his feet Govard took a breath. He had seen her twice now but this was the first time he understood all of what she was. Her black dragon wings edged in living fire. Her fiery red hair dripping in lava. And her eyes, piercing blue and locked on him. The dark Fey beside him warned cautions, as any dark fay should. Nicco, although he should be feared from what he had heard, didn't provoke that intense need to hide. Looking at the goddess, looking at Primitiva there was not a cell in his boy that didn't want to turn and run. Yet he was a crown prince. A skilled warrior , being both kept him from doing so. Dipping his head in a formal bow he allowed his eyes to meet hers. "How may I be of service?"

For too long she she didn't speak. Her nails clawing at the rest of her throne. Finally she closed her eyes and took a deep breath, "You are the crown prince of Arcadian. The advancements your people have created, have not gone unnoticed by the stars. Yet, only your city currently benefits. Is that true?"

A New World

"From my understanding, there are not many who wish to deal in new forms of learning. But the knowledge is there for any who seek it."

Slowly she got to her feet to stand before him, 'What do you need in order to teach those here what you know?"

What did he need? There was several things and he doubted she would know about any of it. "There is many things that would be needed but they are hard to explain without having a way to show you.'

A smile twitched her lips. "Yes I think you are right. When I explain something new I end up creating what I envision just so I can explain it." She paused and looked to Nicco who nodded once. Whatever he had said was only between them, but he agreed. Pricking her finger she allowed a single drop of her midnight blue blood to swell up and linger for a breath. "With this I offer you a gift. You may create whatever you need to advance your work, To teach those who wish to share the knowledge. But the gift comes a price you will never have the free will to turn on those loyal to me." She paused once again locking eyes with him. The whole of the star cities for just a moment being there flickering. 'Do you accept?"

There was no choice. Not a real one. His own loyalty would never allow him from harming one that saved his life. "I accept."

As the drop of blood touched his lips he felt the powers unlocking something deep inside him. Heat and cold colliding under his skin. The knowledge of every scroll he had ever read being as clear as day within his mind. How the new fibers worked. Why each gauge wiring could only do so much. But also how to add the wiring into armor to create shielding.

"Now, show me what you need to teach others."

He shook his head almost auguring that he didn't know how to create it. Yet the room filled up with large spools of cable. Slag to create the metals. Anvils, hammers, tools that he had not yet used but knew that he needed, Everything within the room.

Prim's laugh filled the room, "Alright, fine, we will build you place for all of this . A wave of her hand and everything vanished." Then she retook her seat. "Now, for the real reason you three are here."

Donovan scrunched his brow, "My queen?"

Adjusting in her seat , she leaned back, "Late last night I collected another royal child. He is particularly troubled. I will require the three of you to help work with the boy."

That didn't make sense. He understood why The dark fay and Nicco would be asked but not him. After all he was a little older than a boy but hardly old enough to raise a child. "Um…"

"Govard , you are one of the few fey who were raised with honor. You understand what it means to treat others as equal. Our young friend will need a cool head to help guide him."

Tilting his head in question he finally asked and who is this young prince?"

"The crown prince of Pallas. Prince Griffith."

Chapter 8: Nicco

He waited until Govard had left the throne room. Oh he had been polite but there was not any who didn't know that war was building within the young man's soul. He could see it in in eyes but also felt the range pricking his skin.

But he had waited just long enough for Lord Donivan to find where his query was currently. Waited until he was sure the young Arcadian prince was going somewhere that didn't warrant worrying about his safety. Then he asked the question only he would dare to, "Who is this new prince?"

"Are you asking as a member of my counsel or…"

"I'm asking as a friend. I know you well enough that trouble would not be brought to this place unless it was to prevent something else. But who is the boy?"

For a long time she didn't answer. Which was fine he could and would wait for days if that was what it took to get the answer. And she knew it. Finally she sighed, "Pallas is the center of all of the known star cities. The largest. The ruler. Azia , his rule is to be law amongst all who live."

"And this is the boy's sire?"

"Yes, but more than that the boy has been raised that his word is law. That all others should kneel before him for pay a steep price. His is no older that the crown prince of Osiris but already more than ruthless." Slowly she stood. "What I say now will not be repeated."

"You have my word." And he meant it. There was always some things passed between the first. Others passed to his people. But when his queen asked for his silence it was given.

"He will be a great ruler one day. One of the best among the stars. But never Pallas. His skills once harness properly will be a great assist to our army. To my army."

Taking a deep breath Nicco took a step back, "Alright. First I'll find the Arcadian prince then I'll see how much I need to scare a young lad into becoming a well mannered child."

"Nicco, I have a gift for you."

Puzzled he looked to her. His friend. His queen. Her gifts when not asked for were rare but always needed. 'A gift?"

"Hmmm, because of what I saw… for the moment your poison will not kill our darling prince. But will have the most delightful effect of wishing that it had. Use this gift wisely, I would hate to take it away."

A cruel smile twitched his lips. His poison was deadly but not swift. It never offered a kind death. Those who dies this way took days laying in agony. Fighting fear, fighting their own bodies. The few who had been granted a stay of execution… well even they didn't live long after. Choosing to end their own lives rather than live with whatever memory the poison had left behind.

From the doorway he watched his young quarry paced the room. Throwing what he could lift against the wall. Trying to break what he could. Or trying to find a means of escape.

Little brat. That was thought that came to mind. Should this have been a child of his the boy's backside would already be at least three shades of red. But not yet.

First he would try talking to the boy. Then there was other things to try.

One moment he had been watching with the help of a shadow hidden within the door the next he passed thru the solid wood just as the boy had turned to see him.

"Who are you!" not really a question.

A New World

Adjusting the cuff oh suite Nicco shrugged, "Perhaps you'll earn the right to know that answer. Perhaps not."

Griffith picked up a now empty pitcher and threw it hard enough to break bone , if it connected with a body. Yet it passed thru him in the breath that took to take to mist form and back.

"When my father hears about this…"

His words cut off as Nicco grabbed him by the throat. Taking ever bit of self control that he had not to break the boys neck. But…. OOOO he wanted to. He wanted to hear the bones snap.

And if did Prim would kill him… maybe kill him.

"The only reason you are alive right now is because I will it."

Griffith hung in the air clawing at the hand that held him. His legs trying to find a way to kick the man holding him. Then in one burst of anger was tossed across the room. His back slamming into the dark stone wall. Laying on the floor gasping for air he looked up at Nicco, "I'm the crown prince…"

"There are no crown prince's here. You are a snivelling brat that I can break. The goddess wants you alive. She has said nothing about keeping you whole."

Stuttering perhaps in moment of fear he asked,
"Y-you'd harm me?"

"Harm you? Oh, no my darling. I won't harm you. I
will strip every ounce of flesh from your body and feed it
to my pets, if I want to be kind."

"Lord Nicco?"

The deep voice from the door drew a hiss , "Not now
Donovan.The lad and I were reaching an understanding."

His eyes never left the boy but he heard the footsteps
behind him. Knew Donovan was just steps away. Knew
without a though the dark fey would understand scaring
the little beast into obedience. "Don't break to many
bones. I expect him in training in thirty minutes." the
scuff of boot and he turned to leave, "And Nicco, I think
the Eostre would like to dine of the flesh of a fey before
your pets.Your people might feel slighted."

That got the boy's attention since his eyes doubled in
size, "You EAT fey?"

Standing and brushing himself off, Nicco shrugged,
"Not on a daily biases but if the occasion calls for it.
But ,you boy would be very much alive when I got done."

A New World

He would give the boy time to clean up since he clearly smelled the urine that boy had expelled. Oh there was no doubt in time he would be a great warrior but right now, he was just a child.

Meeting Donovan in the hallway he nodded, "Prim tell you were I was?"

"Nope. Damn shadow dropped me here. Thought I better see what it wanted." he paused, "Would you really feed your pets before your people?"

A deep breath and secrets, "The moment I taste his blood ripe with fear it will cause a slaughter that will only end in my death. For the sake of my people I'll feed my pets first."

"The goddess tell you this?"

"She didn't have to.

CHAPTER 26 · GOVARD

Govard watched from his spot int he clearing. A dirt circle cleared away from trees and rocks. A dome created by the canopy of branches. Large enough for a small army to train here. Yet on the edge of the woods stood Kaida. Dressed in trousers that fit like a second skin. Her white blouse button down enough to draw the eye of any who was seeking a romp. Of course, he would bet any who tried would be dead long before they had anything close to pleasure.

Three young boys were in the center playing some kind of chase me game. The kind that would ware them out before too long. Still they seemed happy and relaxed. Just boys enjoying the day.

Noticing movement to his left he saw Zale approaching. , "Any idea what we will be doing?"

Zale stopped and glanced around, "We , you, Kaida and I have the most formal training. With what was said between Prim and I, we need to be fully trained."

Taking a deep breath he let it out slowly. "War is coming. For too many it has already came."

"Something like that. I have the impression Azia doesn't know those who were in the Void could be given a second life. If he does…"

"Then there enemies among those who were saved." Govard kicked the ground, "I did some checking my guard didn't make it here. And the penalty for lying is a fate worse than death."

"Not you're problem right now. Give Prim time, she'll find him if he's in the Void.'

"And if he's not?"

Zale shook his head, "If Starlis was here I would have an answer for that. Right now… let the Queen rule her flock while we learn everything that we need to survive."

The ground has started to shake. Dirt coming loose at their feet. And rumble of the earth breaking open had all of them scrambling to the tree lines. Yet it was from the trees that came the attack.

Beast wearing armor with swords and shields. Snarls dripping with drool.

They needed weapons. Whatever their abilities were would be no match. Not when greatly out numbered. Govard glanced around the circles center. His mind racing swords , knives … a bow.

As he thought it materialize where he needed it. "There !" he yelled over the grunts and screeches."

The smaller boys ran and grabbed the swords standing back to back ready to fight. Kaida had the bow knocked and aimed. A knife in her boot sheath and a another at her back.

Grabbing a sword for both him and Zale he braced for an attack. Only the creatures didn't move. Their pointed tails poised over their shoulders then dropped from the sky another boy landing in the center of where their backs were pointed.

Back winging Donovan landed glancing around at the creatures and at them. "Lesson one do not assume something is an enemy because it looks different from you. Nor should you assume, someone is a friend because you look the same."

His voice bellowed over the beast. "These fine men and women are Krakens. They are ruled by Lord Ean. Their tails are poison. Of those of this star only one race is more dangerous and feared."

Slowly they appeared. Dwarfed in size by the Krakens. Appearing as fey without wings. Tan bodies.

More lean than muscular. Then Nicco appeared, "These are some of my warriors. They answer to me. Unless we will it you will never see us coming. Your death will be upon you before you know any of my people are there.' He paused looked at the boy in the center of them. "However our poison is slow acting. It's meant to torture you before granting you death."

"And they eat fey." the boy whispered. At that the other three boys dropped their swords.

Understanding this was a demonstration Govard stepped forward, "Lord Nicco, Lord Donivan. We thank you for the demonstration. Perhaps you would be so kind and instruct us in your way of fighting?"

Zale fell onto Govard's bed and hissed, "You have more balls than I do. And none of my sense."

Massaging his shoulder Govard moved from his door. "I knew two things early this morning. One we would be training. And two Azia's brat is here."

Sitting up enough Zale looked confused. "Azia has a heir? And the boy is here.'

"Heir. Brat. Whatever. Since he has been born Azia has been filling the void with more bodies then what he sends to the catacombs. The boy has known nothing but how to be a disrespectful, piece of filth."

"Ah, you should put him in a room with Kaida for a day. He would be the most well behaved child ever." He shrugged, "Wouldn't be able to sit but standing wouldn't be a great option either."

"I'll mention that to Prim or Nicco. But I think they already have ideas on scaring him into obedience."

He snorted, "I doubt they were lying to the boy when he was told the Eostre eat fey."

"Yeah that didn't escape me either. But…" he sat down at the foot of the bed, "Was today a warning or what exactly do we need to worry about?"

"That my friend is the question."

A New World

PART 3

One thousand years before the great war

"I watch as the children grow. So much power, so much promise. Young Magmas is a born leader where Griffith is born warrior. They fight yet they are brothers, yet it is Govard who is the one that so much that has yet to be seen."

-Private Journal of Primitiva

A New World

CHAPTER 7: GRIFFITH

The tavern doors blew open with the heat of anger rolling off of him. "Where are you? You good for nothing, worthless troll slug?'

Everyone who had been their enjoying a meal and drinks put their glasses or forks down glancing around the room. No one moved just watched him. Waiting for either an attach or the village guards to come restrain him.

He knew it. Looking at each of these creations… citizens, he knew what they were waiting for.And Damn it he hated them for it.

Before he could move a hand landed on his shoulder. A friendly squeeze. Then… "So who is it this time Mags, or Zale?"

He grabbed the hand holding him out of reflex not desire to harm the man. "You should not be here."

Slowly the man leaned in, his hot breath on Griffith's ear, "Would you prefer Nicco?"

After a nasty and brief struggle he forced his fingers to relax. Taking a deep breath he turned to the man he thought of as a friend. "Damn it Govard you have more balls then the lot of them." He said as he looked back to those in the tavern. The ones waiting for something to happen before returning to their meals.

A warm smile twitched on Govard's lips, "You haven't answered my question."

Rage bubbled up exploding a barrel of fruit that some one placed outside of the tavern. Splinters of wood, leaves of lettuce and pulp of apples covered the area. Splattered on the walls and street.

Squeezing the bridge of his nose Govard shook his head and muttered, "Shield. How did I forget a blasted shield when dealing with you?"

Griffith took a step back not sure if he should still be pissed off or laugh since Govard was covered in the mess where he was pristine, "Man, I- I'm sorry." it came out as a weak apology since he didn't sound the least bit sorry.

A deep sigh , "At least it wasn't a den of basilisk."

Looking around Griffith cursed,"Shit, we better get out of here. It looks like the guards are going to start some trouble."

"The guards? Damn it Griffith you are a member of the queens guards. The village guards are coming because you exploded the food for the damn Pegasus, Pegasi... whatever the winged horses."

"Winged horses that eat people. You always forget that part."

Govard blinked. "Only Prim's winged beast eat people. Alec had her correct that long before we arrived on this star."

"Then some one need to explain that to Kaida who is the cause of my anger." Before he could finish the thought He smiled at two guards from the castle of night. Their dark polished armor and the seal of the golden dragon was their only warning. These guards could and would put any to the ground before getting answers about the disturbance. Knowing this Griffith smiled, "Gentlemen? Something we can help you with?"

The older one narrowed his weathered eyes. His graying hair could be a sign of age or a sign of fashion. One could never tell when visiting the province of Darke. "General Daegal wants you both at the castle." He paused, then growled, "And the next time you destroy something in any village under my command I will both of you stripped of your commissions. Do I make myself clear."

It wasn't a question. It was a clear direct order that had only one answer. Knowing the answer both Griffith and Govard said in near unison, "Yes sir."

"Now git."

Smiling Govard turned to leave, "Who should I tell General Daegal sent us to him?"

A New World

"General Dayton." The man paused then smiled in way that was not at all reassuring. "I'm sure you know my father, Lord Donivan."

Grabbing Govard's arm Griffith pulled his friend down the street and away from the general.

They were in the land where the village was behind them and the tall dark stone castle before them. It's shadow cast over the rolling hills making day into almost night.

It suited the mood. And the warning.

"Bloody hell, was that really Lord Donivan's son?"

Govard stopped mid step his boot coming down hard on the dirt path. "No one would dare claim Donny as his sire unless it were true. Which only means …"

"Not only does he have the authority to strip us of command but the actual power to strip us of our flesh."

Grabbing Griffith arm as hard as he could Govard asked for a third time, "Now, I ask again. Who the hell pissed you off enough to have that fey and Daegal taking interest in us?"

I doubt Daegal is taking interest because of what just happened."

"Damn it Griffith. You've been a hot head since you fist came here and I have kept you out of trouble more times than I can count. But this can't keep going on."

"No? Then maybe you should explain that to Kaida. And I was in the tavern looking for Mag not because of him but because of her. The darkness only knows he's the only one that she'll yield to." he paused trying to leash the temper that had gotten him to trouble more times than he cared to admit. 'Now lets go I don't want to keep the general waiting."

Under normal circumstance they would have asked any one of the guards where the general was. Any other day would have asked if any one knew why he wanted to see them.

A New World

This was not an normal day. Not normal one bit when Lord Alec was waiting outside of the castle doors for them. His toned arms crossed and the look on his face…

Govard leaned over just enough to whisper, "What the hell did you do to piss of Alec?"

Griffith shrugged. "Nothing I can think of."

Which was true. He could think of a handful of things Kaida had done that might annoy Alec, but nothing to truly piss him off. Not when he was the calm one. The one that rarely had any sign of temper. No, whatever this was…

Sucking in a breath he approached the queen's consort. "Lord Alec?"

Lightning flashed in Alec's blue eyes, "The counsel is waiting." He paused, "Govard, a moment."

CHAPTER 28: GOVARD

He waited until Griffith disappeared down the hall. Meeting with the counsel here? This couldn't be good. And couldn't be just over Griffith and whatever trouble he caused.

Taking a deep breath Govard tried to level he his voice, "Lord Alec? Is there something you needed."

"When you first came here, if I remember correctly, you asked about another fey."

With a nod he agreed, "Yes sir. Talos. He was my personal guard while I lived on Arcadian." Pausing he he tried to think of a single reason that name would be important now.

Tried and couldn't.

Placing his hands on Govard's shoulders, Alec took a breath and slowly let it out. "My anger is not directed to any that live on this star. Know that now."

"Then … what…"

"This will be said by the counsel but I wanted you to hear it from me."

A New World

Govard sat under one his favorite trees. The bark soft as silk, and the leaves that sparkled as light reflected from them. His feet dangling over the edge of a cliff his gaze toward the castle of Night yet he wasn't seeing the castle.

Wasn't seeing anything.

Alec had led him away from the castle out to open land before speaking, "The goddess was in the Void last night. She saved who she could."

'She has been doing that since she had brought me here. So … what…"

His heart stopped as he saw the answer in Alec's eyes. "Arcadian?"

"It fell. Not long before Prim reached them. The ruler of Nexus is here. And others of her kind."

"Talos?"

"Prim has yet to decide if he shall live or if he has a greater reason for being alive. That my boy will depend on what you think."

"Why because of what I think?" he didn't understand. He couldn't.

If Talos was kept during the battle he could have been maimed. Or worse. But the way Alec was being… that didn't feel right.

"Talos lead the army to Arcadian. The battle you witness was because of him."

"No, that can't be… that.."

"Your father was captured that night and sent to a prison of Azia's making. Yet the city resisted until last night."

"Alec…"

"Your father was sent back to Arcadian and Talos used him to detonate the battlement."

He hadn't heard anything after that. Couldn't the ringing in his ears. The vision of what Alec had said. There was only one way to destroy the battlement that way. Only one…

Trying to calm himself he didn't know if he wanted to find Talos and rip him to shreds or grieve. His emotions too unpredictable right now. Too raw… too…

"Mind if I sit down?"

He barely looked over to see the leather boots and black crystal sword. "Mags?"

"Kaida killed some fey last night. A member of Griffith's squad."

"Why she do it?"

Magmas took a breath, "You didn't hear this from me. But Prim has been working with her as a seer. We think she was in a vision when she killed the captain. We can't be for sure why she fed him to the Pegasus." he paused getting comfortable on the edge of the cliff, "Prim wants to talk to you about Arcadian."

"And about Talos?"

"Him too. But she's has already decided his fate is for you to decide. No matter what you have the full support of the counsel."

It was along moment before he spoke, "What does Griffith think?"

"Oh well, you know Grif. Azia wants a war let's bring it to him and be done with it. On top of, ' I demand to be the one to run that bastard thru with my blade.'"

"You're impersonation of him is getting better."

'Yeah well, Prim granted Grif with the honor of killing Azia should he come to this star. Magnar will be overseeing the rest of his training."

The sun was setting before he finally said, "So I guess, I need to see the Goddess about a piece of walking carrion."

A smile twitched Magmas' lips, "You could suggest sending him back to Azia. Maybe with one of those exploding gadgets you created?"

Stroking his goatee Govard smiled, "Make it look like he survived the destruction. Have Prim play with his mind a bit." A laugh slipped his lips, 'I like the idea. But first the bastard has a meeting with my fist."

"Oh here" A club appeared in Magmas' hand, "Kaida says it will hurt more."

A New World

CHAPTER 29: PRIMITIVA

Speaking to the council had cooled her fire hot temper back to what those around her called manageable. Yet, it would take so little for it to spark once more.

What in the name of the creator was Azia doing? Killing thousands. Royal and non alike. Using the star's own defenses against them.

This was not how fey were to act. This was not how the creators wanted them to live. Bloody hell if he read a damn scroll from the time of the Silent Ones he would know that.

But Noooo.

He was hell bent on destroying the seals. Destroying life not only here but where life existed. Her fist slammed on the arm of her dark throne. The sound echoing thru the great hall. "Ahhh."

"My queen?"

Nicco, he hadn't left her side since she left the meeting. Nor would he. "What is it Nicco?"

He took a breath and slowly approached. To many his grace brought out the need to be with him. The desire to share his bed. She had never wanted that for herself, but watching him now… his steps fluid and graceful. A predator seeking his pray. She had seen that look in his eyes before. Seeing it now…

Yes even she needed to tread carefully with this one. At least until his own temper cooled.

"Govard is on his way to speak to you. Should I have him delayed a bit longer."

There, that flash in his dark eyes. He wasn't here to rage war with her, but he would take his anger out on anyone right now. It was in his voice but there was something in the air around them. A warning that pricked her skin…

Right now Nicco was a threat to all that would be around him. All except her.

His temper hadn't gone that deep. Least not yet.

"No, Nicco. Govard has always been the logical one besides Flint. If any of us are to find a solution it may be him."

Turning his head slightly Nicco smiled, "Kaida seems to have joined her mother. Both are currently playing with the poisons that can only be found here." he paused, "Perhaps I should join the ladies."

She nodded. Nothing Nicco did would put the queen of Nexus in any danger. And Kaida, well, even she could scare one of her favorites from time to time. "Very well, but Nicco-"

He waved his hand almost knowing what she would say, "Don't play too rough with Kaida. She's expecting her first bundle of happiness." The pause and smile were at least genuine now, "Thou I'm curious, exactly how drunk did Magmas have to get her before she consented to become a mother?"

"What makes you think I had to get my wife that drunk?"

Magmas came up behind Nicco which should have been a warning. More so since neither she nor Nicco knew he had been approaching. Yet his question seemed more playful than menacing.

Nicco looked to her than back to Magmas, "How did you..."

"Get this close to you without being heard? You are a fine teacher Nicco. One day I might share the spell with you." Then he looked to her, his queen. "Govard, will be a moment, some one he once knew pounced on him the moment we passed."

"Pounced? Oh, my. Hopefully, his temper was steady enough to handle some woman throwing themselves at him."

Magmas shrugged, "He didn't toss her to the ground but wasn't pleased to see her either."

A New World

"In that case, let me go rescue … Govard… the young lady… which ever one may be need of assistance."

Watching Nicco disappear down the hall Magmas gave him a moment before turning to her. "With your permission I would like to stay."

"You have never asked before, so what makes today different?"

"Because, today we know that war is coming."

No fear. No anger. Just a matter of fact tone that he had always had. "Yes, you may stay. But Magmas, what is decided here and now is between Govard and myself, not my generals."

"I didn't think anything else."

Govard strode in not a few minutes after Magmas had made himself comfortable leaning against the window's ledge. His place to perch when he was there to listen but not to comment. Of course that didn't stop him from voicing his opinion after others had left.

Watching Govard she wondered what was said between the two when neither men looked away. Too innocent and much too male for her to deal with.

Letting Govard find his place before her she let her voice be as calm as she could make it, "Alec has told me that you know why I requested you to see me."

Anger lit his eyes but he only responded, "Yes.' He paused, "Am I speaking to the queen or my friend?"

He had good reason to ask. If she said queen he would respond as a general of her army. His anger chained. However, his friend would get the advice she was seeking. "You are speaking to your friend. We will have time for the queen to pass judgment later."

'Oh well in that case…" His posture changed to battle ready and eyes met hers, "I want to speak to Talos, but not yet. I have a request I'm hoping my friend will help me with first."

That was interesting. And unexpected. Leaning forward she smiled, "What request?"

"I would like the goddess Primitiva and her dragon to take me to Arcadian. I want to see what is left of my home."

In all of the years he had never made the request. Never had any of the fey made that request. "Before I answer I want to know why."

A New World

"The blast and destruction after the fires are burnt out… it will tell me more about how it happened and find a way to prevent it from happening again." He pause and shifted slightly, "Maybe prevent it. Either way I won't get those answered from Talos. He was a brilliant guard at one time but he wasn't from my home."

Sitting back she looked over Magmas who had crossed his arms yet had said nothing. "I suppose you want to join us." Not a question. And not a debate about not going. Govard would have heard the answer in the statement.

Magmas stepped forward. "I would. But I also request that Nicco come. There may be places that he can enter that the rest of us may not."

"Very well. General please make the arrangements that will needed for us to leave. And I will prepare Shesha."

Chapter 30: Arcadian

Standing outside the castle of night Govard looked Shesha up and down. Very few times had any of them been this close to the dragon. Very few times had they seem him when not in flight.

Now, standing next to him…

The hand that gripped Govard's shoulder almost made him twitch. "He's grown since last time we've seen him."

Shesha dipped his head in agreement his cloud white scales rippling as he did, "The queen is wise."

"You talk!?!" they both said in disbelief

A laugh behind them had them turning to see Nicco trying to hide the laugh, "You should see your faces."

Pointing back at Shesha Govard gasped, "It talks?"

A snort of hot air was followed by a fiery breath scorching the ground, "I am Shesha King of Dragons. I talk. I also find your people tasty."

Nicco slide up to Shesha stroking his arm, almost comforting a friend, "You must forgive them. They are young and have never heard you speak."

A New World

"Very well I will not eat them."

Heavy footfalls and another voice, "We're flying on a dragon into a war. With no weapons, or armor. Who thought this would make sense?"

"Grif? You're coming?" Magmas asked. His face full of confusion.

"I am not missing a chance to kill the bastard that sired me. Even if I don't have any weapons with me."

Govard saw her approach. Her hair tied back in braid and her dress replaced to something close to leather pants and a tight blouse. This was the queen ready for battle. "My queen?" he gave her a bow as she mounted Shesha without saying a word.

Primitiva looked down at her group. She had seen all of them grow. Now she would see them off to war. Well maybe not war. Not yet. But what they saw now would shape what was to come. "Come, you need not to have weapons while in flight. However, I have your swords and shields should you need them."

Holding onto one of Shesha's spikes that protrude from the dragon's back, Griffith mumbled "We're flying on a dragon. Into the void that kills fey. Hay Govard, Great plan man.. Great Plan. Great f-ing plan."

Govard glanced over to the boy he had watched grow these past years into a nearly unshakable warrior. "Hay Nicco, remember all the times we tried to come up with a way to scare Grif shitless?"

Nicco smiles, "Yeah. Not likely to forget."

"We should have had Shesha take him for a ride."

Both Magmas and Nicco chuckled trying not to really laugh.

Growling Griffith hissed, "Screw you, man. Screw you."

Never looking behind her, yet hearing everything Prim sat a little straighter, "That's enough boys." She paused letting the cold air nip at her skin. "We are close to the Void now."

A New World

Under his breath Griffith mumbled, "The void kills fey. Jump into the void and unless you have a special skill or a carriage it will kill you. Great plan. Really great plan."

Looking over her shoulder Prim hissed, "The Void doesn't kill Lord Griffith it freezes. And you having lived on my star and bound to me are immune to the effects."

Reaching over and slapping Griffith on the back Magmas laughed, "Grif, you might as well strap some steel to your spine and find the temper that has served you so well in the past."

Taking a deep breath he looked back at Magmas, "I hate you."

Just as everything around them turned dark Magmas' smile turned grim. His eyes scanning what the others hadn't yet noticed. "Ah, Grif?"

The faux anger that he had been trying to convey vanished with Magmas' stare. He wasn't looking at his brother he was seeing a fellow general and his eyes were locked on…

Turning Griffith grabbed Govard's shoulder and made a slight nod to the void. The moment was enough to catch both Govard's and Nicco's attention. But it wasn't the king of the Estroe that gasped.

"This can't be just from …" Govard tried to form the words as Shesha glided past the bodies. Children, guards in armor, too many to tell what they had been in life. Or who for that matter.

Prim glanced over her shoulder, "We will brings them back with us. But this is the truth of the Void. What once was empty cold space is now filled with bodies and debris. This is Azia's doing, and his alone."

Govard shook his head, "Not all of his doing. This took help of others."

Magmas nodded, "Aye, others who fall for the false promises and empty lies. And those who stood by and did nothing as their values were chipped away."

Govard stood on what was left of the battlement of his home. The houses and forge were now little more then rubble. Broken, burned bodies scattered the streets. The blood of so many now feeding the star. Allowing for it not to go dark, at least not completely.

Prim came up beside him her eyes scanning for anything and everything. "What do you see, Govard?"

A New World

It wasn't an idle question. Any fool could see the destruction of the war. Anyone could see the senseless loss of life. Looting that had taken place by the victors well after the last survivor was killed.

"The stars cities. Your allies and not need to be told Arcadian is no more. The star needs to appear dark and inhabitable."

Prim cocked her head in question but let him speak.

Seeing a single hand and the ring of Arcadian, Govard knew he was looking at the single most identifying part of his father. Knew the exact point where his father had died to save what he could of their star. "I'm guessing Talos bright my father to this point in the battlement." he paused and took a breath. Later he would grieve the loss of his father right now he needed to be the general that he was and give this report. "That is my father's hand. The placement of the battlement and the creator from the explosion…

… it not near the core. Nor near where munitions are stored."

Griffith slid up next to Govard trying to understand what he was looking at. "This was part of the battlement, right?"

"Yes, but this part…" Govard shrugged, "It was for communication. It relayed news from all over the stars to which my father was allied with. Trade routes…"

The thought formed before he could stop it. "My queen, is it possible that Talos killed the king in order to protect the information?"

"Would you're father allowed for his life to end if it protected his people?"

Govard ignored the question. Something nagging at him. "Magmas, Nicco we need to search the entire city. Look for ways under the streets."

Magmas grinned, "Nicco? I think you could be more of assistance and any of us. At least till you find the opening."

He didn't take orders from anyone but his queen. Would never tolerate an order, yet his queen agreed. It was in her eyes and the slightest dip of her head. For her, and her alone he smiled, "Fine then lets see what is hidden beneath the carnage."

A New World

Chapter 31: Griffith

Watching Nicco dissipate into a fine mist, Griffith turned to Govard. "It's going to take even Nicco time to search the entire star." Turning slightly he looked at Prim, "With permission I would like to get a good look at was done here."

Magmas nodded, "As would I. We might not know what technology is for other than it makes pretty lights. But understanding how our enemies travel. And searching for weakness, now that Griffith and I are great at."

Looking at her wrist and Shesha wrapped around her arm Prim smiled. "Go, the council will need a full report and every detail you can give them."

Almost turning Griffith asked, "Will Magnar be at the meeting?"

"He will if I have to drag him there myself."

A New World

The three of them walked in silence until they couldn't see their queen's watchful eyes. Walked streets that might have been beautiful at one time. Finally Griffith asked, "Ok, since we both know you can temporarily create what you think. Show us what this mess looked like as you last remember it."

This had been a trick to get the boy to behave over the years. Sometimes creating some hybrid monster to scare him. But this was different. This was a general in the queen's army asking for something to better understand the destruction. Letting his eyes closed he thought about every street and every detail that his mind could remember. Allowed the thought to flow over the star . But not in solid form. But more of a ghostly image both able to be seen, yet able to have what was left seen as well.

Opening his eyes, Govard asked, "Good enough?"

Nodding Griffith patted him on the back. "Yeah, good enough." then he wondered off to the nearest building.

Stopping at what once been the tavern Griffith looked it up and down, "Ok, so tavern or meeting hall. We can assume this was empty when the fighting broke loose."

Taking a deep breath Govard thought back, "If we are talking about the battle when I ended in the void, then yes. However, looking at the cabling and some of the exposed wires, I think … " Picking up one of the fiber coils he nodded, "My father won that battle, and they had rebuilt at least some of the city."

Shifting his weight Grif nodded, "We know there were two battles. One eliminated you from the fight. And this last one that destroyed the star. So my question is, what was the king working on that Azia didn't stop until everyone was dead?"

Before Govard could respond Nicco appeared before them. "Magmas, you and Griffith see what you can see above ground. Govard, with me."

There was no arguing with that voice. No, playful banter. It was tone that said now or die. A tone not many would ever question.

"What was that about?'

Magmas opened his mouth and for once no sound followed. Yet he shook his head slowly, before finally croaking out, "I have no idea, nor do I want to."

"Well then, let's go see what we see and report back to the battlement."

A New World

The deeper they went into the city the more destruction they saw. Too clear that survivors had been gathered up and lead to the town's square. Looking at the mangled bodies…

"We stand witness for these dead." Griffith's hand closed into a tight fist. Rage over taking grief for those who had been loss.

"Prim will do something for them. Take them to the Under Kingdom, or entomb them in the catacombs here, But, Griff, I'm not leaving this star till every single Arcadian is in a place of honor."

A deep breath, "Agreed." He paused, "That said, what weapon did Azia have that would kill all of those hear and not have them fight back?"

"Take away their weapons. Promise them life. Promise them the end of their suffering. Come my children, come. The great Azia will forgive you. I will will allow you to live in the gates of Pallas."

They both looked around trying to find the ghostly voice. There not far from them they saw her. Old and tired.

Her thread bare clock wrapped around her, masking what she was.

Keeping his movements slow and deliberate Griffith bowed ever so slightly, "You are a daughter of Nexus?"

She approached not minding the bodies she stepped on. Not caring for how her approach made those before her question her motives. "I am but a spider. The eyes of the queen weaving my traps for those who dare enter."

Oh shit. Nexus had many dark fey. Those who claimed to be spiders were more feared than the assassins. They didn't venture from their holes. Didn't speak to outsiders. Or if they did none had ever lived to tell about it.

"We are here on the behalf of Shivani, and to stand witness to what was done here to these people."

The woman paused. None would use Shivani's name unless welcome to do so. In truth, very few know the name of the Queen of Nexus. "Very well young one. I will not preserve you for the queen."

Thank the darkness for that. " Can you tell us what you know? It will be beneficial to mount a defensive."

Turning she waved her hand. The square being swallowed in a cloud of green mist. The last thing Griffith heard before his world went dark was, "You should live it for yourself."

A New World

 CHAPTER 3: ARCADIAN

Fear slammed into him. Anger over took him. How much longer could the fighting last? Too many light cycles. So many dead.

Another explosion.

This one closer. Time was running out. But what could he do? He was just one fey. Just one voice amongst thousands. No one would listen to him. Not his children who had gone off to fight for the king. Not the ones who sided with Azia.

Bothers were fighting brothers. Family against family. Each side trusting theirs would be the victor yet not seeing the destruction left in their wake.

The food was running low. The children dying in the street choosing to be killed at hands of the enemy rather then to stave in what was left of their homes.

Taking a deep breath he readied himself to fight. If he was going to die here, it would be to defend his home. He was no coward. No, he would not die as one.

His hand touched the slab of rock that was blocking the door when the whole city shook. The explosion sent a wave of dust thru the streets and what was left of the homes.

A New World

He had no idea how long had had been in his home concussions. No, idea what had happened. Yet moaning he gathered his wits.

Somehow, he was alive. Not really injured just sore. To that he was thankful.

If he had been a youth he would have charged out into the street. His instincts kept him still. Kept him quiet. No one was looking for him. None would think to check the destroyed houses for survivors.

Keeping his movements slow and quiet he lifted the stones from the doorway. Just enough to crawl thru. Just enough to see it was dark and the solders of Pallas were in the streets dragging people from their homes.

Too many being forced towards … the square , it was the only place down that street. At least the only place other than the palace.

Barely breathing he heard the soldiers talking. "Make sure they aren't armed. Too many have explosives."

The other one replied, "What do you think Azia will do with the survivors?"

"They either join Pallas or die."

Waiting until the street was quiet he kept to the shadows. Kept out of site. He needed to see. Needed to hear.

Getting to the square he watched. Every living Arcadian was there. Not many. Only a few hundred out of the thousands that had been here just days before. Thousands from the millions that had been left since this war had started.

Then he saw him. The gold and red robes. The thin frame. Azia. The king of kings here on Arcadian.

They had failed. They had lost.

Still he listened.

"Great people of Arcadian, I come to you as your leader. Your king. I come offering you food and salvation. Medicines to treat your wounded."

Somewhere a woman's voice, "At what price?"

Azia laughed, "Ah, to the point then. Bind yourself to Pallas and forever live within the golden gates of the city or remain here. No other city will come to your aid. None will care if you parish. Right now my loyal ambassadors are in every city telling their leaders that it was you who are the cause of their problems. That is was Arcadian that was responsible to the debts that now have." he paused. "Think wisely for I will not wait long for an answer."

Azia turned and started down the street. Stopping briefly beside a guard. A cruel smile touched his lips. "Kill them. None here have the strength to feed the gardens of Pallas."

CHAPTER 33: GRIFFITH

Fear. Rage. And grief slammed into him. Choking he clawed at the ground trying to get to his feet.

A hand grabbed him. Swinging out his sword he heard the whistle from the speed then the hiss that only Nicco could produce. "You damn well have an explanation."

Ah bloody hell. Coughing, wheezing he managed to croak out, "A spider was here."

No response. Then, "Magmas said the same thing when I woke him and dragged his ass back to the dragon. And I would like to know how one spider can render two trained generals on their asses?"

Finding his feet he didn't think about what he was doing. Just shoved Nicco as hard as he could then shouted. "Not a damn eight legged thing that Prim finds amusing. Spiders belong to Nexus. They weave traps for pray. And could have damn near killed us before even you could get here." Coughing he paused. Needing to get his breath. Needing to give a report that wouldn't have Lord Nicco going for his throat.

"Look, man I'm sorry about the shove. The spider shared a vision."

A New World

Nicco crossed his arms and waited, "Magmas woke in the same manner. Pissed off and battle ready. Only he had enough sense to tangle with me over what was seen."

Griffith turned. Not a smart thing to do if Nicco was truly pissed, but he needed to vent some the rage. Tossing out his hand part of a building exploded revealing the body of an elderly fey. One that looked to have been starved to death and not killed with the rest.

Pointing his sword, "It was his last moments that I witnessed. And I'm telling you now, Azia will die by my blade."

Magmas was sitting on the ground with his back leaned up against Shesha. Parchment floating before him as he wrote.

Griffith paused. Magmas cutting into an enemy was common. He could vent his anger out for hours that way. Magmas putting his anger to paper? Ah, bloody hell , he would rile the entire army before the anger was smothered. "Mag."

He looked up. His dirty blond hair dripping in sweat. And rage… the fires of Osiris burned deep within them. "That bastard needs to die a slow and painful death. His screams need to be heard in the depths of the Under Kingdom. While his flesh is melted from his body."

"Well hell, finally we both agree on something." Griffith smiled. He wanted to rage but now that his own rage had cooled, he was no match for Magmas. At least if they played fair.

After taking a seat near Magmas, Griffith leaned back. He appeared relaxed. Only a fool would think it was true. "So where is the queen? I think we have enough information to keep everyone busy for a while?"

"She and Govard are under the city. There is something there to make the star appear dark from the outside."

Since Magmas wasn't looking up when he said it, there was no choice but to sit and wait. IF the queen needed them, Nicco would drag them to where they needed to be.

But for now, they waited.

Calling in a peace of parchment of his own, Griffith started to write all that he could remember. All the while hoping never to cross another spider. At least not one from Nexus.

A New World

CHAPTER 34: THE COUNSEL OF THE FEY

Govard took a deep breath and let it out slowly. Soon he would be summoned thru the tall wooden doors into the heart of the castle. Soon he would need to explain the countless fey that the queen had brought back on this trip.

The ones that now lived in some form among those in the under kingdom. Those who were housed in the castles after being given some form of life.

And soon he would pin Talos to the wall and get the rest of the information that he needed before he decided if his once friend would life or die.

But right now he needed to calm himself. Needed to focus.

His eyes fixed on the tapestries of battles won long ago. Few knew the truth of these battles. Outside the counsel and perhaps Zale and himself, most of the fey warriors believed theses creatures were normally hidden away. Or controlled by some form of confinement.

A New World

No, it wasn't true.

Prim had created these monsters in order for the army to have an enemy to fight. Ones that grew and learned from past. Learned how they were attacked and others defeated making each battle harder. In turn each of those in Prim's army gained skills otherwise not used. Unlocked abilities very few ever heard of.

Oh if the battle got too heated Prim would intervene. But she was a good queen, she understood that her people needed something to do that gave them purpose but also trained them for the war that one day would come to this star.

A cough from behind him.

The door hadn't opened. No sound of footfalls. There was only one person who could come in that quietly in a hall with only two points of entrance. "Lord Nicco?" he said as he slowly turned to him.

"The counsel is ready for you." Nicco paused and his brow scrunched together for just a moment. "I would like you to explain something before you go in."

"Alright?"

"The contraption. What does it do?"

Govard snorted, "Do? Hell if I really really know. My grandfather said it was the future of travel. Taking a fay from one place and transporting them to another star."

"Is it possible Azia has something like it now?"

Anger came back to Govard's eyes, "If he does then there is not a star city that is safe."

The double doors opened ans he prepared to enter. It was strange he and Zale had been close to Prim since the moment they had came to this star. Yet, neither of them were members of the counsel.

Magmas , Flit, and Apollo. The sons of Osiris sat together to the queen's right. The first as they were called, Prim's favorites sat to her left. There was an empty space next to Flint then Magnar a scowl on his face.

Nicco slide up beside him, "Foot of the table. Magnar will behave."

Taking his place at the foot of the table he waited as the queen adjusted in her seat. Her galaxy blue eyes focused on him as she softly spoke, "Lord Govard, thank you for meeting with us. The counsel has made some decisions that will not be debated on."

A smile twitched his lips, "I don't recall debating any of your decision , my queen."

She sat back her eyes moving slightly to lock on to Magnar, "No, you have always been wise enough to know when to argue and when to hold your tongue."

"May we discuss Arcadian and Talos?"

"Talos is yours to deal with however you see fit. But, from what I know for fact, the machine we found on Arcadian was the reason your father gave his life where he had. Stories of how the weak were left to defend the star when the worriers were taken away , are already being told to the other cities. Should you return, you and you alone shall know the truth of Arcadian."

He nodded. When the goddess asked for him to keep some information secret… well he would take it to his death and beyond. "One day I would like to see my home rebuilt."

"One day Arcadian will have a new ruler, but it won't be today Lord Govard."

His eyes lowered. No, it wouldn't be today. Nor would it be him that ruled. But she had given him a gift. One that he would hold onto for as long as he had breath in his body. "In that case I would like to propose we formally name the army of this star."

Magmas leaned in just a bit, "And what does Lord Govard wish to name this army?"

"The dragon army."

A New World

"The war is coming. What is fought here is just a battle. One of many. Lives lost now… only some will be truly lost. Others,they will be needed for what is yet to come."

-Private journal of the Queen of Nexus

A New World

CHAPTER 35: PRIMITIVA

Primitiva sat on her gold and magma throne. Her Castle of Fire was quite almost too quiet. Gone were the children running through the halls laughing. Gone were the heated augments of her first.

Each now protecting those that only they could. Alec should be safe in the Castle of Night. Should be, didn't mean that he would. If one person told Azia who he was... what he was to her… his life would be forfeit. His power no matter how limited would be absorbed by the filth that called himself Azia.

Her fingers curled around the armrest. Too tempting to destroy him here and now. Destroy him as he entered the outer most layer of her star. It would solve nothing. No, she had to play this out. She had to show the Fey that it he alone that was killing their children. He was the one hording all of the power for the Star Cities for himself. Moreover, it was he alone that had started this war.

Lava bubbled out her window. The sound echoing throughout the halls. Another bubble or was that an explosion coming from the Star Cities. She could know for sure.

Another thought. Ari. Her Ari. The only child she had ever given birth to. The child that she had waited so long to give Alec. It hurt her heart to know she may never see him grow. Never see him ever be the Fey that he was meant to be. He would grow and learn all that he needed. He would one day be released from his present form. She had seen that. As she had seen that, she would not be the one to release him.

Would Alec know what she had done to insure the life of their child?   She did not know. She couldn't. There was much still clouded in mystery for her to know what the full outcome would be.

A pain lanced her heart from the thought of losing him. The thought of losing both Alec and Ari.

She would not shed the tears that burned her throat. She couldn't. Azia and his army were on their way to her star. Not by way of coach that would have been expected. No what was worrisome was each flying here on their own accord. Each navigating the void in hopes of being the one to destroy her.

Something had changed. Something horrible. Something she could almost point her finger at.

If she had to bet, it was because of Bradwr. He had aligned himself with Azia. He wasn't worthy of being an Eostre. He wasn't loyal to anyone but himself.

Her anger grew not at him but herself. She should have killed him many light cycles ago. Alas, it was too late to rectify that now. He was bringing the enemy to her door. And with them he was bringing deaths to countless others.

With her eyes trained on the large double doors of smooth black stone she calmed herself for what would come through that door. Resigned to be the powerful queen that her people needed.

Resigned herself to act with the honor that Azia had long ago forgotten. A breath then two… Someone was coming. Too fast to be a page or even a messenger. Whoever it was, they were strong. Their natural powers were that of …

The doors blew open with a crash. Magmas not the boy who she had raised but his father… stood in the doorway panting. His golden red wings covered in many shades of blood. Testament of those he had faced in order to come here. His fire red robes that marked him as a royal Fey little more than rags hanging from his body revealing his metal armor that had been made for him. From where she hadn't a clue. The smell of smoke clinging to him.

Flames danced wildly in his eyes.

Slowly she rose from her seat. On the star of the Silent Ones, they had been equal. Here, she was Queen. Here he would yield to her or be destroyed. Her temper already too close to snapping to tolerate any disobedience from anyone. Even an ally. "Magmas, why have you come?"

Taking a breath, he took a knee a sign if surrender to her "The bastard Azia is on his way here. One of your people sought him out and gave him the means to travel throughout the void without the need of carriage. Those who would side themselves to you are now trapped within their own Star Cities." Magmas took a shaky breath. "None of those who had been holding the void survived his attack. This will be the last star to see war. I'm sorry Prim, I have failed you."

"Oh, stand Magmas you oaf. I have known for some time the war would come here. I had hoped to buy more time but … It matters little now." She turned watching the lava creep up the sides of the castle soon it would spill over the mountain taking all in its wake.

Her people knew this day was coming and had prepared for it. All of the homes that would be destroyed were already empty.

Her people already carefully hidden within plain sight. Others posed for open attack while, others… Well she didn't have play with all of rules of Pallas.

"You knew?" Slowly Magmas got to his feet tossing aside his tattered robe. "You have prepared for this?"

"I have. Even since Bradwr left this star to seek Azia out I have made changes."

His eyes watched lava slowly rise past the window. "You seek to destroy this castle?"

She turned sharply following his gaze, "Oh, the lava will expel from the top of the mountain. We are safe within these walls. As there is also another way out should I need it."

Catching his breath, he nodded, "Those you had patrolling the outer ring of the star have fallen. It is their blood I wear now."

"Oh, they are of little consequence."

"Prim?" Worry filled his voice. Fear that he had sided wrong.

"They were already dead Magmas. Most for more than a century. Their remains will be collected and returned to my other kingdom, there they will either pull themselves together or choose to

remain … dead does not sound right. I have yet figured out a word to describe them."

"They were… why would you send them…"

"Magmas, I do not send anyone anywhere they are free to decide for themselves. Now come. I was expecting a report from a messenger seeing you have more information then he would… you will join me with meeting with my generals. There is much to discuss."

A few steps and she was at the door her fire red hair braided down her back. Looking ahead she said, "Come. We shall join my generals in my war room. I will show you what I know for certain.

Then you will tell me what you know. Together we will figure out a means to an end." She just hoped with that end she didn't need to destroy everything that she had created. Hoped when she unleashed her power that she wouldn't wake the Silent Ones.

With Magmas trailing behind her, Primitiva stopped hallway down a long corridor. The out wall made of white stone the inner side made from crystallized lava. "Do you find my castle interesting, Magmas?"

"It's unique." He hesitated, "But from a defense stand point is it safe?"

"I assure you that out of all of my castles only one is safer. But that one is too close to where I wish to draw Azia near."

"Prim, Azia is smart he won't go into the open unless he must."

"I know. It is why I will give him little choice. Come my generals are waiting."

Magmas stumbled back a step seeing what she called generals. Their races he had no names for. One nearly as tall as the room itself muscles the size of boulders. Eyes of black coal. And the spikes that protruded from his body. He could almost feel the poison that each carried. The rest of the chosen warriors… each looked more frightening then the next. Each he had no doubt would tear apart a Fey with nothing more than a moment of inconvenience.

"Generals, this is Lord Magmas he has been leading our efforts within the Star Cities." Prim paused as she glanced at him, "We no time for proper introductions. Now shall we get to work?"

The one who was the tallest nodded, his hand over his heart swearing allegiance to his queen. "The pillars have all been destroyed."

Carefully she took a seat at the head of her large rectangular table. As she did the rest of her generals took their seats along the sides. "Good. Then Nicco was successful speaking to Gwydion. What else?"

A New World

The one that had the feel of a dark Fey stood up from the table and called in a map. Slowly he unrolled it, "Here…" He pointed to a spot on the map near what was labeled marshland covered a wisp of mist representing her dark veil; "… what is now farmland. We have declared the bones of the fallen enemy to be taken... With no disrespect, those who are loyal to you my queen do not wish to live for all eternity with the enemy."

Prim nodded in agreement, "If this is the will of my people I will allow it. The bones as they free themselves of skin and tissue will be made into structures. I leave the details for those structures up to the builders. I see no reason to restrict their creative ideas." She paused for but a moment. "Are all of my castles placed on alert?"

"Yes, my queen. Several of your dragons are attached to each. Shesha is now roosting near here as the lava has now become too unstable for him to land within his tower."

"And they are all watching the skies?" Another question she didn't need to hear the answer to but Magmas however did.

"They are. None shall attack until the enemy has fallen. As requested Castle Golden Light has been vacated. The town's people have all taken shelter deep below. The entrance sealed up for the moment." The Dark Fey paused, "Is there a reason that castle has been more or less emptied?"

Slowly Prim locked eyes not with her general but with Magmas. Licking her blood red lips, she smiled. Not her friendly smile that most welcomed but a smile that chilled those that were in the room. "General Daegal as I understand why you are asking that, I will answer but it will not be repeated beyond this room."

With a tip of his head General Daegal retook his seat. "Of course, my queen."

Setting back, she steepled her fingers together. "I have conceded both Castle Golden Sun and The Castle of Glass."

Magmas stood up trying to find the markers for both of the castles. "Prim?"

With a flick of her hand tiny castles appeared on the map. "The Castle of Golden Sun will be used by Azia for the moment. As it is most like the Castle of Pallas. It is imperative that we push the enemy to a place that we can control. And away from heavily populated areas."

Shaking his head Magmas said, "The rules of Pallas are clear…"

"This is not Pallas not is it a Star City. As I will concede to some of the rules of war I will not bother with those that only apply to a Star City."

A tense deep breath and Magmas slowly let it out. "I apologies, nothing like what you have created and are now defending has ever been …"

A New World

"Actually, Magmas there is evidence that once all of the Star Cities were at one-time part of one collective entity. But that is for a discussion at a later time. Right now, we need to keep or focus on defeating Azia."

"It will not be as easy as that. Whatever Azia has backing him his fighters are now stronger than any Fey that I know. Nothing we have seems to penetrate their skin."

Prim nodded once, "I will assume Bradwr has given Azia a sample of his blood. If he did then it may act like a temporary shield for the enemy. However, the brat wouldn't know that it would only shield those from weapons from the Star Cities. Those that my people carry… And I mean that to include those who have fallen and have decided that they will fight for this star… They now have weapons to break that shield. Once the shield is broken…" the rest trailed off with her shrug.

"My queen?"

"Azia will attack the most populated cities first leaving the villages for last. He does not know that any place he chooses to attack is only filled with trained warriors. As it stands today we out number his forced by nearly ten to one. Once his attacks fail in this area…" She pointed to a place that now sparkled with light, "Those who are hidden below Castle Golden Sun will attack. I have given them a device to watch each battle as it unfolds."

Still looking at the map Magmas shook his head in disagreement, "Azia will stay, and fight."

"No Magmas he won't. Azia is not a strong as the Star Cities think he is. His natural abilities are not even a tenth of what they should be for being born to Pallas. His son on the other hand if he had been leading this attack then things would have been different."

Magmas narrowed his eyes, "He leaped into the void some time ago." Almost remembering the day, he heard the news. And like then figured out Prim had collected him from the void.

"He did and was raised by me. He is truly gifted and nothing like his father. One day he will be a good leader. As it stands he is posed to lead the resistance near the City of Night. He has also asked to be the one to accept his father's surrender seeing there is no honor in attacking my star."

General Daegal stood up, "My queen if we are done here I would like to join the major."

"Of course."

It wasn't until they were alone Prim got to her feet. "Magmas you have been quite for much too long."

"I'm looking at your map. There is a lot of ground to cover between each city. So many places for Azia to attack that wouldn't fit with your defense plan."

"Azia is arrogant more so then any Fey and he seeks revenge which makes him stupid. In every city in every village there are only warriors. Those who can't fight… those with no ability to do so or children who are much too young to see the gore of war are all protected deep with the nearest castles. "

"It is possible that Azia or his forces will find them or destroy the castles themselves."

"My darling, only a creator with greater power then I can destroy the lower sanctums of the castles. True the visible structures can be destroyed but nothing can touch the lower buildings. Nor can anything penetrate the rooms without being let in."

"You sound sure in your ability."

"I have tested every ability of every Fey that has fallen against my defenses. I have also tested the ability of all of those that I have created and their people. In addition, I have granted more power to a select few including gifting them the blood of an Eostre. None have been able to withstand my defenses. In fact, the only reason they lived at all is because I so willed it."

Magmas wiped his mouth hiding the fear that had chosen the wrong side. The fear that the creature that sat before him could and would destroy all of the Fey. "You could stop this before another drop of blood is shed."

Prim sat back her eyes focused on something far beyond this room. Far beyond this time. "No. If I unleash my power… all of my power… I will unleash a greater threat then Azia. I alone cannot defeat that threat. Least not yet. The one who will be needed to help me won't be born for more years then I can see. But I know her name. And only her name not what she will look like."

Leaning forward Magmas stayed silent for a long moment understanding the threat that she worried about. Worried if the Silent Once may still wake because of this war. Choose not to speak of them but instead asked "And her name?"

"Nisha. The daughter of the night. The conqueror of the Silent Ones."

A New World

 CHAPTER 36: AZIA

Azia smiled as he took a deep breath of the sweet-smelling air. It was different from any Star City. More than that, it was a worthy conquest. His deep soulless eyes scanned the area. Not a soul in sight. Just Objects that he had no name for. Deep browns with green sprouting from its appendages. A sea of green dotting the ground. Buildings made of some kind of pale cream stone.

More stone this one white and round creating a wide path. Nothing here he could name but everything soon would be his to rule.

Slowly Bradwr formed beside him glaring at the empty city. "There should be thousands of people filling these streets. Or their bodies littering the ground." He turned slowly desperately trying to find a single soul. Trying to find anything of flesh and blood. There was nothing. Not even some vermin scurrying to its home. "Something isn't right."

A cruel smile formed on Azia's face. "It is custom for a ruler of a Star City to house the attacking Fey in a safe and luxurious home. In most cases opposites of where they are housed. It gives both sides the advantage of watching the battle." He paused watching his slaves … his army… falling to the ground. Each taking a knee waiting for his intrusion. "Come I would like to see this place before I decide if it is worthy to house me. Even for a short time."

Bradwr narrowed his eyes and hissed, "You underestimate Primitiva and those who follow her."

"I underestimate no one. She is nothing that I have not killed before. Her kind has been bred to feed the catacombs. To feed Pallas and nothing more. Now come I would like to get this little pissing match done with and collect her powers for my own. "Then I will destroy the star that had created such a fowled creature. With its destruction I will destroy the one I had thought to possess. The creature known as Avyanna.

It wasn't a house but a palace made of sparkling white stone.

It's highest tower reaching more than a dozen stories. Windows facing wherever a battle could be fought. "Marvelous. Perhaps you should have come to me sooner."

Still looking for any sign of life Bradwr hissed. "I do not like this. She conceded an entire city. For what purpose? Mark my words if you trust what is before you then you are a fool."

"Why should I trust her when I have you to distrust everything for me?"

"She has destroyed the pillars and I cannot find any of my kinsmen who side with me."

At this Azia turned. This boy had promised an army. Had promised a weapon that could destroy his brother and those that were bound to him. And yet he had yet to produce anything other than meaningless words. In a deep growl he spat out, "Explain."

"When I left several scores of my people had pulled away and hidden themselves. Nothing could have destroyed them. And none could have been found by any but me. There is no one stronger then myself among my people." Slowly he changed back into his mist form trying to find any of his army. Trying to find anything to point to where they might be. What he found was chilling. Changing back be stumbled back a step. "They're gone."

Azia's narrowed into tiny slits. "So, you have no army." "They were destroyed. Not even a sliver of bone remains. I

do not know how this is possible. It shouldn't be possible." His brother should not have had that kind of power. And their grandfather was too old and feeble to kill anything larger than a mouse. This should not have been possible. It shouldn't have been. He was the most gifted Eostre… He was… Gasping for a breath he gathered himself, "But you have an army. The trolls will fight for you as well as all who live in marsh. We should attack all of the outer cities at one time. Divide her army; make them attack the smaller villages while we attack her most prized places."

For a long moment Azia considered what is ally was suggesting. Using his army of what was called trolls and others would spare the Fey army, but would draw out the creature Primitiva. "It sounds reasonable. Show me what you are thinking."

Closing his eyes Bradwr nodded, "There is a room near here with a suitable table and enough chairs for your leaders. I should be able to find a large map."

"Fine. We will meet in one hour. There is a pet that I would like to play with for a time."

Waiting for Azia to disappear down the stone path and back to where the Fey were still waiting Bradwr hissed to himself. "Filthy beast. As soon as this is over I will dine on his flesh…" Greed lit his young face as he imagined ruling not only his people but all of the known races.

The room was long, pale cream stones with gold wisp formed the high walls. Soft red fabric covered the floor. A long rectangle table made from the brown object outside filled the room. Chairs formed from crystal lined either side of the table. More than thirty if he counted. An adequate amount for those who would lead the Fey into battle. A large golden throne at the head of the table. Blood red fabric for the seat.

No other Star City had dared to leave him such luxuries.

None dared to presume he wouldn't have brought his own belongings to show his power. None had dared to suggest he couldn't feed his army by leaving troves of food in the stores.

She was infuriating. Worse yet his army were taking notice.

Insolent creature. Who did she think she was? How dare she undermined him by leaving houses filled willed with furnishings for his army. How dare she presume he need her cache of food. He had half the mind to burn this city to the ground.

And would just as soon as she was captured. Just as soon as he could peel away her flesh just to hear her shrill screams.

The door behind him opened as Bradwr slipped in carrying a rolled parchment. "Are your trolls ready to attack." Not a question but an order. He wanted to be done here before the creature could turn his army against him.

"They are. Your leaders are waiting outside." Bradwr paused, "Should I retrieve them?"

A wave of his hand and he took a seat on the cursed throne.

Might as well look like he had brought the furniture. Not likely anyone would dare question him. Not when he would make their death painful and public if they did. "Show them in and let us end this."

As the last royal Fey gingerly took their seat Bradwr unroll the parchment letting it cover the entire length of the table. Names had been carefully scribbled onto the map already. A moment later several colored stones appeared. Turning to face Azia, Bradwr asked, "What color would like to represent your army?"His fingers curled into a fist as he hissed. "The clear ones you fool."

Bradwr narrowed his eyes. For a tense moment he didn't move. Didn't dare to. His rage at being spoken to in that tone was almost enough to forgo this alliance and devour everyone in this room. If not for needing their help in seizing control of the Eostre crown he wouldn't even bother with them. In a low hiss he responded, "Watch it old man I'm not one of your pets that you can speak to like that."

Quickly Azia got to his feet his hands slamming down on the table showing just a small bit of temper. "You will show me respect, boy."

A slow smile reveling several rows of sharp teeth bloomed on Bradwr's face. "As long as we are allies in this I won't kill you. I make no promises for those who follow you."

He had no way to kill this creation no way to defeat Primitiva on her own territory without his help. And no way to rule what would be left should this boy turn against him. "We will call a truce for the sake of defeating the fowled creature."

With a nod Bradwr set up clear crystal stones around the Castle of Golden Sun. "This is where we are." Clusters of black stones and a hand full of silver stones covered the names of the other castles. One gold stone was placed at the Castle of Fire. "The gold stone is Primitiva. Her warriors are represented by the black stones. The silver are winged serpents. They are fierce fighters if in the sky little more than a small nuisance when on the ground. They are slow and too large to move very quickly. They are easily killed from behind.

Now the other villages should be attacked first. We need to cut off the food supply for the castles. It will draw out the warriors so I recommend the trolls and those of the marsh attack first. They are many in numbers and some are skilled fighters. After the war is won they can be easily dealt with. One of your Fey may be able to penetrate the city of Glass. Once inside they should whisper honeyed lies to turn the people against Primitiva. It will crush her to know the people she tries to protect would rather fight for you then live by her rule."

One of royal Fey, A female with short brown hair and silver colored skin raised her hand to be noticed. "My lord, are we understanding after this battle is won those who help are to be killed?"

It wasn't Azia but Bradwr that answered. His tone bored and irritated that he had to explain anything let alone answer mindless questions. Questions that he saw as beneath him. "Trolls are fonder to start with. They fight because they have no reason not to. Either way they will die. The people of the Marsh however have no alliance to anyone. Make no mistake if you do not destroy them as soon as the war is over there will be nothing to stop them from destroying your kind." Not that it was true. The people of the Marsh all had some ability for most it was so minor it wasn't even considered an ability.

He paused waiting for anyone else to ask stupid questions. "Now here…" he tapped a placed called the castle of Glass. "This should be where your troops are in greater strength as well as here… Primitiva's private meadows. She will stop at nothing to defend both."

Getting to his feet once more Azia stared at the map. "How many does she have within her ranks?"

"Not more than twice your number. And none have my blood to keep them safe."

"Very well, we will do this your way." For now. Azia paused before greed lit his face. "You said the creature has a child."

"Her consort would know where the child is. The Castle of Night would be the most reasonable place for him to hide within. "Bradwr paused considering what he might be able to do providing he could find someone to help him. "I may have away to draw him out. If I succeed you can hold him as random. Or at least pretend that is what you are going to do. After all, out of all of her elites he is her favorite."

Azia waved his hand and smiled, "Very well bring him to me. He will die the moment the creature shows herself to me." His smile grew more sinister as he said, "She will watch as I destroy him so completely his blood won't even have time to fall to the ground."

A New World

CHAPTER 37: PRIMITIVA

Exhaling slowly Prim sat back in her throne tears running steadily down her cheek. It had begun. The war that was needed to   rid the Fey of Azia. Still the loss of life wore on her. Many she could bring back but they would never be the same. The life that they once had… the memories of who they were … would all be gone. Everyone around them would remember them and expect them to be who they had always been. But the truth was they would never again be that person.

The blood that would fill their veins would no longer be the life blood of their ancestors but that which she gave. The exception was those of per Fey blood. The Fallen as many now called them. They could be reborn… recreated… and still be whole. But her creations… those who were descendants of them… it would never be.

It was kinder to let them go. Still it did not help the ache that she now felt stabbing her heart.

Her eyes closed as she tried to regain some composure.

Tears would have no use today. No use until Azia was no longer in power. Then she could allow her tears to fall. Allow herself to mourn the loss of so many lives.

She heard the heavy stone door drag on the floor. Heard the shuffle of boots, too many to be only one person. Too quickly her eyes were open pinning each of those who dared bother her when she so deep in thought. For more than a breath she held, each of the heavily armed men not recognizing any of them. A moment more and she knew they were they to protect her not harm her.

Still it begged to question who had sent them. Getting to her feet she glared at the one closest to her. A dark Fey. Not someone to disregard lightly. "State your business."

Her voice was much colder then she would have liked but right now what she was picking up from these men was troubling. Still it did produce a noticeable wince from the man.

Slowly he took a deep breath, "Word was sent. We are to keep you here until the Azia has been dealt with."

No there were here to kill her, just not yet. No, they needed her alive until Azia and his army was slaughtered. But who had sent them? That was something she couldn't seem to find. Or they simple didn't know the Fey who was now pulling the strings. It didn't matter. They would die the very moment they moved against her.

Retaking her seat, she made sure she had the look of a queen. Made sure her gaze couldn't be matched by anyone in this room. The very calmly smiled. It must have worried the men because the scent of fear now filled the room. "This is My Star City and No one has the authority to give orders as to my whereabouts."

"We have orders…"

"I don't give a damn about your orders." Her voice boomed throughout the room rattling the windows. Nearly breaking them and allowing the lava to flow inside. "This is my castle and I give the orders." His voice quieted to a soft whisper, "Do I make myself clear?"

The dark Fey squared his shoulder but didn't back down, "You may rule this rather large star but you do not rule the true Fey. You will yield."

Yield? She was the goddess Primitiva she did not yield to no one. With nothing more than a flick of her finger all of the guards were thrown against the far wall before crumbling to the ground.

The sound of bones snapping echoed through the halls. Several of the men screamed an arms and legs broke from unseen forces.

More screamed as their wings crumbled as easily as parchment.

Stepping over to them she knelt to the leader. Knelt in front of the dark Fey. Her smile now cruel and vicious, "Now, do you really think I will yield?"

"I will see you dead." He gasped out.

A New World

A quick motion and his neck snapped before she stood. "Pity, he had such great potential." Glancing over to rest of the broken weeping men she hissed, "Anyone else have something to say?"

A dark mist flew into the room before forming. Nicco glanced around at the males before dismissing them completely, "My queen, I need a moment if you would allow." Asking was a courtesy since he could see something treacherous in her eyes. Something that he was sure that he didn't want to see unleashed.

"Follow me Nicco. And have someone collect these pathetic excuses for Fey. I would execute them but that is a fate too good for them."

Oh yes something had pissed her off. But that was something that he and the rest of her first could deal with once the war was over. Or he could deal with after she was somewhere not in this room. "One of my people has heard something. And Alec thinks he understands the meaning." He glanced over at the Fey that now lay silently on the floor trying not to look like they wanted to scream out in pain. He flashed them a glimpse of his teeth taking his tongue to each of deadly pints before returning to his conversation, "It involve the Fey King Magmas."

Prim turned sharply to him her fury almost too hot for her to control. Something outside this room was pressing on her and wasn't the battles she had already seen. It was something more. Something that she would need to deal with. Something that she could not name. Lest not yet. "What about Magmas?"

"Alec and I agree he may be using you to rid the Fey of Azia in order to rule Pallas for himself."

A quick mental thought then she shook her head regaining some of her normal control. "Oh. Of course, he will rule Pallas. I have decided this many seasons ago. The Fey are in agreement. He will rule the Star Cities and I will rule here and rebuild what is being lost." She turned hearing a loud screech. A scream. A sound she had never heard before. Yet Nicco didn't seem to hear it.

What was it?

A footman ran down the hall coming straight toward her. One of the few of lizard like people who choose to live under her rule rather than live in the marsh. Stills she didn't know his name. "What   now?"

"One of your chained creations broke loose. She has found traitors within the castle."

Ah. Her banshee. Well a modified version of it. She could hear the screams as a warning she was attacking something. But none others would unless they sought harm to her… it's master. "Very well. She may do as she sees fit. Have their bones taken to the designated sight for the unworthy." Then to Nicco, "Come with me. We will speak in a more private place."

Storming into her private sanctuary Prim slammed the heavy wood door behind her knowing Nicco would follow. Knowing he would wait until her temper simmered down enough to be approach with whatever he needed to say. Slowly black mist started to pool together then just inside the door Nicco materialized his head bowed slightly. Taking a deep breath, she held it before creating a soft overstuffed chair. Her long dragon like wings vanishing as she sat down. "Now tell me what you wanted to say but couldn't in front of the soon to be rotted flesh."

"I understand there are things you haven't been able to tell your counsel however neither Alec nor myself trust Magmas. With the Fey now openly attacking you He may try to do something to remove you once you defeat Azia."

For several long moments she sat there debating what she should say versus what Nicco expected her to tell him. Realized he only expected her thanks and nothing more. He wouldn't argue with her about what he thought should be done. Wouldn't waste his time nor his words when he could just as easily take care the perceived threat and seek forgiveness later. Finally, she closed her eyes choosing not to look at him as she spoke. "Magmas is no treat. He needs me alive for as long as it is possible in order to hold the Star Cities and insure that the changes that need to be made can. Also, Magnar is to rule Osiris once this war is over. It was a condition that Magnar sat. Avyanna will join him on Osiris. Starlis will rule my home star, as she should have all this time. If I am injured at any point Magnar will destroy Magmas and rule over Pallas.

However, that does not mean he would not try to make me his bride. He knows well enough I have the power to rule the whole of Pallas and the Star Cities and still be able to rule here."

Nicco nodded. "You could have told your counsel. We worry about you…" Suddenly he paused and looked out the corner of her eyes listening to something that only he could hear.

"Nicco? What do you hear?"

"That Fey have changed their plans. Ones that you have saved are now attacking our people. The Castle of Glass has fallen to Azia." Again, he paused trying to make sense of the information that he was receiving. So many voices all speaking at once. Images flashing deep within his mind. "Your meadows are destroyed. I – I think they are organizing to attack all of the castles not just the cities."

A New World

Taking a deep breath Prim squared her shoulders. "Then it is time for Azia to meet the Queen who he had left alone."

CHAPTER 38: PRINCE

MAGMAS

The bubbling of the magma in the pool just feet away was the only sound other than his quill leaving ink on the parchment before him. Even his brothers lounging on the soft red couches weren't making a sound. No, they were waiting for him to respond to the reports from those under his command.

Each one more grim than the last.

Fey that had been sent to this land so many light cycles ago were becoming uneasy. Many were skilled warriors with no war to fight. Others … those with the gift of foresight… those were the reports that clogged his heart. The words they sent…

Oh war was coming but even they couldn't say for sure who would win. Just too many variables. Too many unknown factors. Oh the signs were all there.

A gift from the gods. A power not yet born. Rage and lies. Dragons of old. Vultures devouring the lands once rich with life. Death where it should be safe. A few told of his undoing yet assured him it wouldn't mean death but they didn't understand what it meant.

To ask Prim seemed so easy. But with her babe on the way. Her own temperament was too predictable. Her powers, her abilities flaring to frightening heights.

No, there would be time to ask what worried him. He just hoped putting it off that he wasn't missing something in the process.

Setting his quill back in the ink well he turned just as a large bubble of magma popped in the pool. His eye lingered for too long on his brothers. Flint had his own command yet most of his troops were better suited for carrying messages. Apollo? His troops were mostly feared. Even if he, the namesake of the kind of Orisus, commanded the bulk of the dark fey… his brother commanded those who were born of true fey and those only found on this star.

No Apollo was no fool. Neither were those under his command. Still they needed to know what he did. Later he would speak to Lord Donivan and find out the rest.

With his eyes locked on nothing he softly spoke. The words weighing heavy this time. "War is at our door steps, I can feel it like a shadow darkening our land, or the blood that flows through my veins. Prim has done all that she can to prepare us. To prepare those who will fight to save what is left of the Fey race."

For a long moment neither of his brother's moved. Finally Apollo sat up letting his feet slip into the pool just in front of the long red couch. "Yes, she is doing everything she can to protect us. Every day she adds to the defenses. Freya has been stalking the halls making her own suggestions."

He nodded once. Freya. Not under Apollo's command but having that of her own. She was the ears and blade of the goddess. Alive? One of the dead? No one really knew. Part dark fey part… they didn't know what she was. But it was all agreed upon that the darkness had more compassion than her. And more mercy.

A grim smile twitched Magma's lips, "I pray that it will be enough. I pray that I will once again see our home. I pray that I can take my family there to bathe in its rich lava pools".

Apollo shrugged, "Me too. I do miss our lava pools. This one… I rather luke warm. This is almost comfortable for me. Although I'm sure if Prim was asked the temperature could be changed."

Flint leaned back and shook his head. "What do the seers say? Or is the great general not allowed to tell his brothers?"

A sideways glance at the youngest of them. Silently he pulled his dragon handled short blade from its sheath. For a moment he studied it. How many battles had it already seen? How many more before this was over? "I will never see the sunrise of Osiris again. The star will survive but it's not my place. And none have been able to say more than this war will carry a deep price but it won't be the end."

Pushing up from his seat, Flint looked down to his bare feet. "Well then, I guess it's time to set the royal houses in order."

"Flint?"

"We have royal fey from every star hidden within our ranks. Zale from Obsidian. Mag, you knew he was royal since you married his sister."

"I did. He's a pain in the ass on his best days but there is no one outside you two and Govard who I would trust to watch my back."

A careful nod and Flint continued, "Govard, no one knows that he hailed from Arcadian. The technology they hold there is more impressive than weapons from Obsidian. Yet as of yet they have not chosen a side."

"Don't forget Griffith."

Both Magmas and Flint glared at Apollo. But it was Magmas that cursed. While Flint smiled, "He's family Mag. Not by blood but he has your back. Push comes to shove he'll do more to fight for you then against you."

"Yes well, it's a good thing he's adopted. I do not want to think of him as a brother. But I will admit his skills in battle are close to my own."

And that was all he would concede to the son of Azia.
At least till the butcher was killed and this war was over.

A New World

Chapter 39: The Goddess Primitiva

Three thousand years ago, I came to this land in hopes that I would never again see any from my home. I had hoped to create a world where there would never be a reason for needless bloodshed. A world where my actions would never be seen as less then noble.

I see now that it was nothing but a fool's dream. For only a fool would keep all of her power to herself and never seek to change those who ruled unjustly.

Yes, it was a fool's dream. Yet I am no fool.

I was born for a reason, and that reason was for greatness. This world that I have created is proof to that. One day, all who ever knew me will understand that. Sadly, that day is not today.

No today, I am forced down a much darker path. Today I am to be the goddess Primitiva and all those who witness my power will truly see me as not the kind protector of this land. But as the weapon that has been kept sheath for far too long.

A New World

Today, my greatness will come at a great price and with much bloodshed. For now, this will be my legacy.

Setting her pen to the side of her writing desk Prim gazed at her words. Only a heartbeat and they would be dry. Another and she rolled the parchment up and sealed it with a black blot of wax. Her eyes closed as she held out her hand to Nicco. "Please take this to Karnack. It is to be placed with useless scrolls. One day it will be read. And one day what happens here will matter."

Nicco took the scroll and swallowed hard, "What are you to

do?"

Shaking she slowly stood from her writing desk. "What I

should have done all along. I am going to destroy the threat to my people."

"I will join you…"

Not looking at him but rather keeping her eyes tightly closed she put every ounce of authority that she could muster into her voice, "No, Nicco. This is my final order to you as the queen. From this moment I can only be the goddess. Do you understand me?"

He had been her trusted advisor for more centuries then not.

Of her first he alone knew the true depth of her powers. Powers that had always terrified him. Not because of what those powers or abilities were, but rather what it would mean should she need to use them. "Of course, goddess. I am yours to command in any way that you see fit."

Tuning slightly to him she swallowed hard making her choice. "I want you to go to the endless sea. Take your wives and live with Princess Sedna and her people. As long as I draw breath, so shall will you. Your brothers should find a place among their people

hiding in plain sight. The day will come when their strengths and talents will be needed, but not today. I will do what I can to protect those who belong to me but I cannot make any promise that I will succeed."

Breathing deeply Nicco quietly asked, "You are preparing for the finial war?"

"I am preparing for the day when the queen of darkness will take her place among the great Fey… now please…"

Before she could say another word an Eostre warrior materialized before her. "Goddess, my lord … "fear lit his hunter gold eyes as he looked at both of them, "I have just received some grave news."

Nicco nodded for the man to continue before taking his place beside his queen.

"King Magmas took Lord Alec out of the Castle of Night. It appears he told Alec of the problem, that has arisen with in the village of Glass. I have not yet found out how the Fey King would have known before any of us."

Prim shook her head and looked at Nicco who looked just as puzzled, "Problem? What problem and why wasn't I told about it?"

Hearing not only concern but anger in the Goddesses voice the warrior changed to mist form for only a breath before once again standing before her, "The village has ordered that all of your warriors are to leave their village. They have all decided to join with the Azia."

That was more than a little problem but one that she could correct easily enough. Closing her eyes, she spoke correcting this messenger as to the other problem so that the rest of her warriors would not make the same mistake, "Not the Azia, just Azia. It is his name not title."

Soothingly Nicco rubbed her back, "It is not of importance of it is his name or title. But what is however is why the human village has sided with him."

Opened her eyes Prim straightened her back, "No Nicco it is not. Least not yet. They have no power to harm any of the warriors nor have any weapons that could sway this battle in his favor. They are of little consequence at this time." Her eyes then locked on the messenger. By his heavy armor she understood this was no mere messenger this was one of the off spring of both the blood of an Eostre and of a dark Fey. A highbred of both true Fey blood and that of a creation. One of few that would breed life into the blood lines that would be needed in the true war. This was a man who would be more then dangerous in the coming years.

But this too she could not worry about. Not now.

Alec was the only thing that mattered. The only one of her first that she had not been able to see a clear line to his destiny. The only one she could not be certain would live in the coming moments. "Tell me about my consort and what else you know."

"It is not clear if Lord Magmas is truly working with Azia or if he is working for himself. Either way… Alec is now in the hands of Azia as his prisoner. They are now at the Castle of Glass." He paused no longer able to watch the anger and pain dance within the goddess' eyes. "Those near the castle can hear lord Alec's screams. None have been able to penetrate the castle." Once again, his eyes opened, "I am sorry my queen. I know not what can be done to save him."

Rage built inside her hot and violent. Death would come to any who had harmed her beloved.

… Beloved. A word she had never used to describe Alec before. A word she now wished he had heard her say to him. A single word that she now hoped he had felt even if she had never said it.

A New World

"Nicco, see to the preparations I have already gave
you. I will deal with Azia. Do not send another soul to the
village nor Castle of Glass."

Nicco bowed his head slightly before dissipating into
the air around her. Even if he didn't show it the pain of
losing his brother even just in thought was already more
than he wished to bear.

"My queen?"

Taking the few steps over to this man she let her
fingers caress his face. A singe touch and she knew all
that she needed to know about this man and the strength
that he had yet to grow into. "You have given me all that
you could. Now it is time that I give you what I can."

"I don't…" Her finger pressed against his lips
preventing him from uttering another word.

"Shhhh, my little one just listen. The day will come
when my daughter will bare a child of flesh and blood.
When the time is right you are to become her mate. When
Magnar returns you will tell him this. He will know you
speak of what I have seen." Slowly Prim closed her eyes
then whispered softly into his ear, "You will stay here.
You have seen enough of this war."

Once her finger left his lips ne blinked unsure of
what to say.

Finally decided on the only words that he could find.
"Thank you, goddess."

"Don't thank me my child. The path you will walk is a dangerous one but it will be rewarding. This I swear to you."

Before he could speak anther word she slipped out of the room and disappeared down the endless hallway. To where he would never know, yet he knew whatever was to come he had earned the favor of the goddess.

For years she had been flying over these valleys and rolling hills savoring in the beauty. Always finding solace in the calmness of the open terrain. Never had she imagined the bloodshed and carnage that would cover her home. Her eyes scanned the countryside hoping to find one corner that was left untouched by the hands of this war. Yet she could not.

Not in the far north where the shores met the endless sea. Not to the east where the trees were so dense that only the Eostre dared to dwell. The far south was little better with its wet marsh trapping the Fey who had foolishly dared to land in hopes of claiming that terrain for themselves. No, there was not a single crevice that was left untouched.

Too many explosions shook the ground sending shock-waves   through the air. Her gorgeous fur covered trees now ablaze with unnatural fire. The flames would probably be seen within the Star Cities. The fires would be a beacon to those who still had not arrived. Beacons that their flawed King was winning this war.

Her anger grew as she saw firsthand the cost of the war.

She had to do something. She had to…

"No!" She screamed in rage. Her meadows. Her sacred place that calmed and soothed her. Azia's army was destroying it. Her Army would never step foot there, understanding this as a sacred place. As her place.

No more. No more would she allow her home to be destroyed by these carrion eaters. No more would she allow them to assume that she was weak and their chosen king would win this war.

Her rage boiled over threatening to spill out over and consuming her people. That she would not allow to happen. Instead she focused her rage, her anger on a single target.

Her meadows and those who would destroy her home.

Those who would harm her people.

Hovering high above them she called upon all of her dark power. Called the power of those of her Under Kingdom. Called upon the powers of those who had bound themselves to her.

Dark mist covered her. Streaks of white and yellow swirled within the black. A single bolt of power plowed down on the Fey before they had time to react. The few that had felt the power drawing near had tried to escape, tried to flee before the power consumed them. Their screams forever imprinted in the now blood-soaked ground. A layer of fine black dust… sand now covered what once was soft grass and white sand.

She could find another place to find solace. The land too contaminated now by the blood of the enemy. Too contaminated by her own rage.

Still, it felt good to rid the realm of these Fey. Felt right to let her power run without censor.

A grim smile formed on her blood red lips. Azia wanted to meet her and all of her dark unrelenting power… well he was going to see why her people called her the goddess. He would see firsthand why creators were gods.

A New World

Hovering over the City of Glass she saw everything. The people holding what meager weapons waving them at her. Holding them in a way to say they were against her and wanted to see her blood run freely within the streets.

Later she would deal with them. Later she would find out what she had done for them to turn on her so. But not now.

No. Right now she had something more important to do.

Using her power, she let her voice to be carried over the land. She knew it would be heard in every corner of her land just as clear as if she had spoken the words to each of the cities individually. "Azia, show yourself you coward."

The castle was still a way off but she could see the high balcony clear as if she was standing a few feet away from it. Azia with his thick red robes hiding the fact that he was ill and not far away from death. Bradwr standing behind him clenching Alec by his wings almost tearing them from his back. And her Alec barely conscious from the pain they had already inflicted on him. His golden blood dripping from several cuts that were visible.

She could see his armor had been melted away from his body. Could see the blisters that the heat had caused. Could see his sun kissed hair had been pulled in clumps from his scalp.

They had done a great harm to her consort, now she would pay them back in kind.

Flying closer to the castle she paused seeing the nearer she drew the more pain Bradwr was causing her consort. Her Alec.

From this distance she would never be able to free him.

Slowly Azia smiled as she glanced over his shoulder at his prisoner. Then he began to clap as he started to speak. "Have to finally decided to succumb to your destiny, creature?"

Her voice took on a dark tone that even surprised her as she growled, "Let him go, Azia."

As Azia narrowed his soulless eyes he smiled as he assumed that he had the upper hand. "Or you'll what? Destroy me? Try and he dies by your hand. No, my dear, you will surrender to me."

A New World

Alec blinked once then looked up at her. A single tear ran down his dirt covered face. He didn't' need to speak for her to know the truth. The only thing keeping him alive was Bradwr's hand that she could see now was not holding his wing but rather was plunged deep within his chest. A single squeeze and he would be killed.

Unless Bradwr used his poisoned nails to rake across his heart.

Both were a possibility. And neither would he survive from.

There was nothing that she could do to save him. At least nothing until he was beyond their grasp. Then… oh then she could do something. She could give him a second life.

She had the power to do it. And was going to use every ounce of that power to save as many of her people as she could.

Knowing this she let a smile form on her face as she laughed coldly. "You think killing him will make me submit to you. You? Do you not know who I am, Azia? Do you not yet realize what I am?" She bent over laughing as she still hovered in the air. Her laugh ringing out over the land.

Angrily Azia hissed, "What is this? Boy…"

A slow cruel smile formed on the lips of Bradwr. Without saying anything or giving any hint of a warning, he turned to a dark mist swallowing his prey. When it rescinded he used a single small sliver of bone to clean his sharp pointed teeth. "Pity you have no use for your former consort. He made such a pitiful snack. Although he was had a rather delightful taste."

He devoured Alec in a single heartbeat, and there was nothing she could have done to stop him. Nothing she could do nothing to bring him back.

She wasn't laughing any more however Azia was. The malicious bastard who thrived on the pain of others. How had he become so twisted, so corrupted to condone what Bradwr had just done? Didn't the fool realize that the boy would do the same to anyone? It didn't matter if he did or not. All that mattered was that she knew the truth of what Bradwr was capable of doing.

Blinking everything felt surreal. The pain that was now lancing her heart should have been a killing blow yet it numbed her. The smirk on Azia's face, a matching one on Bradwr's young face should have sent her into a murderous rage. But for the moment she just blinked letting the realizing that nothing that she did now would bring her Alec back to her. Nothing that she did would give Ari back his father.

It wasn't until she felt the tear run down her cheek that she had even realized that she had been screaming. She hadn't realized that she had been reaching out her hand preventing Bradwr from becoming solid once more. It wasn't until that moment when time once again mattered. It wasn't until that single tear had dropped from her chin she felt the unbearable pain from losing the only person that she had ever really loved hit her with its full force. The only person who she had ever wished to see at the dawn of every morning. And the last person who had ever wished to see before she allowed her eyes to close.

He was gone now. Her reason for being was gone to her.

Rage started to flicker deep within her. Rage so dark even those who thrived on pain and suffering would find the depth of that ire shocking.

Catching her breath, she saw the look of amusement on Azia's face. Saw him nod to someone. Just before a she could find the person that he was signaling, a cluster of arrows whizzed in the air. Several bolts whizzed past her head creating a whistling sound. Not just simple primitive weapons that the humans still used but ones that had been spelled. Some even had been dipped in poisons that were common within the star cities.

Shouts of anger from well below her. Slowly her eyes focused on what was drawing her attention.

The humans. Those without any Fey blood. All of them actively trying to fight not just her but also the Fey who had come to her aid. Several were in the low rooftops vigorously trying to shoot their primitive weapons at her. Their betrayal was the very last straw… the last reason for her to remain bound to her own rules.

The last of her grief turned to dark brutal rage. Why had her people turned on her? What had she done to deserve this? No, it wasn't what she had done but Azia had done. This was his doing.

And he would die because of it.

She was not just some Fey that Azia could control nor kill. Her rage bubbled over as she channeled the true depths of her power. She was a creator, but not just any creator, she the most powerful that had ever been born since the first Fey came into existence. More than that she was a natural born warrior. She was the Goddess Primitiva and there was no one greater than she.

Suddenly with her rage the normally stark gray sky tuned dark almost becoming twilight. Fire of black and purple flames surrounded both the city and castle. Lightning poured down striking several of the crystal houses melting then to the ground.

Her power ran freely now along with her rage.

Azia the corrupted Fey was laughing her. She could see in on his face. He should be cowering.

It didn't matter he would be dead soon, as would those who had turned against her.

A wisp of fine white mist surrounded her. Information being passed to her. Her castles… all of them were being attacked. The buildings themselves were showing signs of collapsing. The Castle of Night had already fell trapping all of those who had been beneath it in the under rooms. There was no word on those who had still been above defending the castle. No word from her dragon force.

This ended now. Azia had taken her love. He had destroyed her home. But worse of all he had destroyed her Ari. Her child.

Summoning all of her power… all of her will… She let a single large bolt of power plow into the city of Glass. The blast sending a shock-wave back to her nearly knowing her from the sky. Rocks and debris being sent from the earth and into the sky above. The cloud of dust spreading out over the land.

It would cling to the air for hours. She had the power to settle it but she would not. No, that would be a kindness that those who died this way did not deserve.

Flying higher she looked at the destruction of her prize city. No longer did she have a city made of ice and crystal. No longer, would there be a race that she called human. No longer could this land be used for life. Nothing would ever thrive here again. Her raw power now filled this land tainting it. No, it was her rage that now tainted the land.

It gave her little gratification.

It was then something else hit her. An emotion that she had never felt before nor could she name.

Looking around at the now large crater that had been blasted deep into the earth she saw alone figure standing within it center.

Still enraged that something survived she flew down ready to grasp the figure. Ready to rip it a part with nothing more than her brute strength. Almost upon it she saw it was not a person but something that was made completely of mist.

Slowing now, she back-winged to land. It was then she saw the child that she had named. The man who was the King of the Eostre. He was no longer alive. Nor would his people be. No, they were now what was called a Shade. A race that only existed in her Under Kingdom. "Gwydion?"

He raised his hand to keep her from speaking. "I knew the risk of coming here. The death of my people is solely on my hands."

Seeing him. Standing within the crater where so many had died… she nearly broke… she…

It was then Magmas landed beside her looking triumphant.

Arrogant. "We won. With Azia's death the rest of the Fey surrendered."

Too many emotions collided within her. Joy wasn't one of them, nor should it be. A quick motion and she faced the arrogant Fey king and growled, "Won? Damn you. Look around! NO BODY WON!" Primitiva screamed. "You might be the next ruler of Pallas, but make no mistake… no one won this war."

Either not understanding or not caring Magmas shrugged unconcerned with her little outburst. "Are you or are you not a creator?"

Without thinking, her hands grabbed his throat. "You…" "My Queen, Stop." Gently Gwydion pulled on her arm trying to get between her and the new Fey King. "Let us mourn those who cannot be brought back and help those who can. This Fey…. Is not worth your anger."

Letting go she stepped back and spat at the feet of Magmas.

Spat on a man who she had thought of as an ally. "I don't know how but you are responsible for the death of my consort. His blood is on your hands."

CHAPTER 40: THE COUNSEL OF THE FEY

Dawn was just creeping over the mountains. The bridge between the light and darkness. So it was fitting to be having this meeting on the cusp of either. Zale had been found with Govard both had decided to help Griffith. With what to be exact neither would say. Still they would be here shortly.

Pushing the heave double doors open he paused taking in the room and those held inside.

The counsel normally had the five favorites of the goddess.

Her generals. But always the Queen herself.

Magmas paused in the door way of the chosen meeting room. The Queens chair was not at the head of the table. Only Nicco and Donivan were already seated.

A New World

Nicco looked ready to be sick. His long narrow
finger tapping restlessly on the table. And Donivan…
There were reasons dark fey were feared. And his
aurora …. one wrong breath and those who had survived
the battles of yesterday would not survive him.

A simple gesture with his hand kept both of his
brothers from speaking. Just that one silent command and
all three of them slipped into the room without making a
sound. All three all too aware of the dark eyes that were
watching them.

Pulling out his chair Magmas nodded to Lord
Donnivan.

Slowly the dark fey eased back in his chair. " I won't
kill you for being born of that…"

Nicco reached over grabbing Donivan's arm, " Not
now. There will be time to let your anger loose. Today is
not the time."

A jagged deep breath, "You're right. It's not. But I
will enjoy tearing that bastard limb from limb."

Slowly the door opened as Magnar strode in his face
that of stone. He didn't speak as he took his seat. His eyes
hard and unforgiving.

"Magnar…" Magmas started to say just before the
council doors blew open and controlled furry walked in.
Griffith. His temper more than hot. Behind him Zale and
Govard. Both looking ragged and darting looks of

uncertainty. Looks that translated to *Don't expect us to hold him back.*

Nearly to the table Griffith tossed a golden blade onto the table. "We spent half the night finding that. The bastard was trying to sneak off with it."

Magmas took a quick look at the blade. His heart ached. The anger of the room now he understood. "Alex…"

Speaking through clenched teeth Griffith growled, "Dead. We assume the same for Ari." He paced the length of the room needing to move. "Azia's death was too kind."

Nicco looked up, "No, it wasn't. But it was too quick. But we will not ask the goddess to recreate the bastard just so we can take turns ripping him to shreds."

His eyes looked around the room there was more going on here than just the death of Alex. General Degal wasn't there. Nor several others. Ean. "Is this …"

"Lord Ean has the task of hunting trolls and others. He's not needed here. Degal… is with the queen. As is Shesha." The others were not mentioned. If they were alive or not, only the goddess knew.

Nodding once Magmas adjusted in his seat. "Very well. Magnar. Will you please …"

A New World

His knuckles cracked his eyes locking on Magmas, "Let me see your blade."

Confused, he laid it on the table not sure why Magnar wanted to see it. But he resigned himself to whatever was going to happen.

Magnar let his hand hover over the blade, his eyes locking on Zale. "This was your father's blade?"

Was it? He hadn't seen it since … he blew out a breath and closed his eyes. Recalling the memory of the last time his father had showed it to him. The last night he had been on Obsidian. . Slowly his eyes open. "That's the blade of Obsidian."

Magmas started to protest, "If it's the blade of your father's you should…"

"OOO no. I was never meant to wield that blade. Nope. Prim and I discussed it all of once. We agreed then the blade would decide who would rule Obsidian." He paused… "Magnar? Do you agree?"

Magnar grunted then growled, "Boy, no blade will decide who rules…" His hand clenched the hilt. Just as his fingers wrapped around the handle a jolt of raw power bubbled around the blade destroying the table and blasting everyone away from the table…

… Everyone but Magmas.

He looked around and tried not to smile. After all smiling right now might get him killed. But he was the only one still in a chair. And the blade had came to him in the moment it had… well he wasn't sure what it had done but made itself known.

"Are we done discussing the blade?"

Too many sets of eyes watched him. Undeterred he slid the blade back into it's hilt. Anyone looking at him would swear that he was calm… it was a good thing of those in the room on Magnar might pick up on a stray thought. And his brothers no… they wouldn't dare look beneath the surface.

Magnar narrowed his eyes but let out a breath. A wave of his hand and the table and chairs were once again back. Once again remade from the rubble that had been left. Leaning forward in his seat , He let his arms rest on the table. "We will agree now, that until Prim's successor is ready to rule that I will be her voice."

There was no agreement needed. Magnar wouldn't have said anything if it hadn't been discussed already. Magmas nodded once, "No one will argue with that claim."

"Good. It will save me from breaking your bones." Magnar paused, "Prim will remain in the Under Kingdom. For the Star Cities to have a chance to survive it is best if the Fey forget about her. Flint, you and Karnack are the words smiths. Think of something."

A New World

He looked down at the table and swallowed hard, "Mag and I discussed some of it last night. It will take a while to rebuild this star but it will give us time to come up with a suitable story."

"Fine. The traitor king will take his fey with him by the sunset tonight. I granted them the use of the dragons to carry them back to their lands."

Nicco hissed, "Will the dragons return or finish what they started?"

"Prim will recall them to the Under kingdom.All but one."

Magmas shuttered, not "Khaalida"

"Would you wish your wife to be without her namesake?"

Damn Magnar he didn't need to sound so cheery about it. The fact that his darling wife didn't know the beast name… or the fact that she was the the mate of Shesha… "Are we certain Kaida can control the beast."

It was a valid question so why was everyone glaring?"

Magnar ignored the question his eyes locked on Magmas, "In the meantime, You and Zale are to return to Obsidian."

It was tempting to argue but there were things that needed to be put to rights there. Far more than those here." Fine. What about Govard?"

Govard leaned back in his chair, "As far as I know the star where I came from is gone. You have no need for any of my skills here."

"Unless you count attracting more women than Nicco as a skill?" Apollo coughed from under his breath.

"That has never been proven. However, I would like to visit the great forge of Obsidian. If Magnar agrees."

For a long time he didn't move. "You will remain within the Star Cities held by the counsel. Which one I don't care."

Magmas narrowed his eyes. Catching the phrasing, "You're preparing for war… Not a battle over a single star. But war"

"The new ruler of Pallas has shone his true colors. Make no mistake the war that is coming won't end so quickly. And it will be on his hands."

A New World

CHAPTER 44: PALLAS

The star should shine like gold. The gardens lush and vibrant.

Houses and buildings of pale cream stone. Streets lined in gold with the citizens filling the street to welcome home their new king.

This is what Magmas has pictured in his mind. What he had prepared for. This… this destruction… what had caused…

The polished buildings were nothing more than burnt rubble. The castle with the hanging gardens … only the door to the catacombs was left standing. Around it… he wouldn't call the rubble mounds of pebbles.

The gardens were gone.only bloodied dirt remained. And the citizens?

He glanced over his shoulder. There were those who had survived the final battle with Azia. A few scores that had come from this star and wished to return. But not enough to …

A New World

His anger seething and he turned to one of the dragons. "I wish to speak to Primitiva…. Bring her here now."

A snort of hot air melting some of the rubble. Melting the gold that was left in the streets.

He barely jumped back in time from that burst of hot air touching him. Now thankful that he had… Still, "I demand to speak…"

The words were not finished as he was knocked to the ground. The man who stood before him seething in anger. Dark eyes. Dragon wings. And full of rage. "The goddess has no wish to speak to you. I'm free however."

"Who are you?"

"Magnar. And make no mistake you're only alive because the goddess so wills it. If up to me …" He let the words linger in the air.

Understanding the threat , Magmas slowly stood, "How am I to rule when there is nothing left to rule?"

A cruel smile filled Magnar's lips. "This is the price of your foolishness."

"This…"

"Did you really think when she unleashed that burst of power that it was contained to just one star? " Magnar leaned back and laughed. "All of the stars that sided with

Azia now look like this. The others… " Too quickly he grabbed Magmas by his throat, "Those stars now belong to the counsel of the goddess. Except Lunaista. That will be ruled by the spawn I sired. They will not be ruled by either Pallas or the counsel."

That was interesting. This creature was leaving a single star to rule… itself… oh the possibilities. "And if I …"

"Interfere with that star and I wouldn't just kill you." He pushed Magmas back to the ground. "The star will remain neutral for three generations. Then it can choose."

So many things would need to be rebuilt. But Prim was being sentimental. One star could not tip the scales that much. One star…

He would have to do this slowly. Give aid as a friend. Yet it would take a while but he knew two things… One was there were legendary weapons that needed to be found. Not many but whomever controlled those could rule much more than the known stars. And Prim didn't leave anything to chance.

A New World

No he would have his pet. He would have her powers for himself. But first he would need to be the fair king. The one that was different for Azia. He would need to build trust and his armies.

A choice … Call all of the Fey here to rebuild the capitol or… a smile twitched his lips. No, Nexus. The dark star. Their warriors fierce and placating the dark fey… yes that was where he needed to start.

"Whispers are coming from the shadows. The King of Obsidian has been chosen. Arcadian has fallen. And Nexus? Only a fool would dare challenge the un-dead."

Private scroll of Kalaraja, general of Arkrsna

CHAPTER 4: OBSIDIAN

They arrived at the gate of Obsidian without the needed fan fair. Too much would need to be done before the people accepted an outsider as the King. Laws …

Oh sweet darkness… the laws he would have to read over before deciding on which to keep and which to do away with.

Magmas let out a soft moan already thinking of the mounds of paperwork.

Zale smiled all too knowingly. His hand resting on Magmas' shoulder, "I am so glad it is you and not me who carried the burden of that sword."

"Yes well you don't have to sound so excited about it." Magmas paused… "After all since you were born here…so, I'm making you my adviser while I rule on Prim's star."

Govard coughed back a laugh seeing the dismay on Zale's face. "You don't have to be a seer to know that was coming."

"Since when do Star Cities have advisers?" Zale whined. Not that he really minded but being the older brother to the king he could get away with it.Or more to the point the twin of the queen.

"Come on. I would like to see the city before I decide to see the castle."

Embers floated in the sky. Warm wind gently teased the air. The smell of wood and magma lingered.

For just a moment Magmas paused. His eyes slightly closed as he savored this smell. A strange contentment falling over him. His mind relaxed… a feeling teased his skin…

His head turned ever so slightly to the side. There was something beyond his hearing. A feeling.

Two steps. The ground shifted beneath his feet. His hand already gripping the hilt of his sword.

"Mag?" Zale's voice. Filled with worry.

"Magmas… what…?" Another voice. Not worry now caution.Govard. Yes that is who that voice belonged to.

Another step. The air changed around them. Something more than smoke hung in the air.

Sweat. Rage.

One more step.

He didn't need to turn to know his friends were behind him already looking for the first signs of trouble. Looking but not seeing.

His blue eyes flashed open. The sword of Obsidian slashed through the air. An arc or white light coming from it's blade. The sound of steel connecting with steel.

Stunned gasp. Armor clambering.

Finally his eyes focused. Dozens of trained warriors still battle ready. They must have been spelled in some enchantment to get this close. To get where they had them surrounded.

Yet….

Narrowing his eyes Magmas growled, "Your men kneel , yet you…"

A New World

The gaze of the guard fell upon the blade. Then to Zale. "You command a sword that few ever controlled. Yet you leave the offspring to the former still standing."

With hard unforgiving eyes, Magmas' hand tightened the hilt of the sword. Vines of black wrapping around his arm creating a bracer of mist. His rage at the insult burning…

Zale slid his golden sword into its hilt carefully letting his hand rest on Magmas' shoulder. Then he laughed, "Ah, why would the king kill me? His most trusted adviser. Besides, he would have to deal with the queen's fury for the connivance."

Zale's words were enough to push the rage to the side. At least for a moment. "Which queen are you referring to?"

"Does it matter? Kaida you know would very well voice her opinion and I doubt Prim is in any mood to settle squabbles."

For a long moment Magmas let the words linger in the air. Let his eyes tell this guard how deep the insult had sliced. Then a forced smile. "Come on Zale, you know this star better than I." A heartbeat of a pause. Then to Govard, "I suppose I'll find you at the forge?"

"Hmm. Something tells me whatever is coming I'm going to need the best in the way of armor."

Walking past the men Magmas didn't dare look down to them. Later he could meet with those here. Later he would learn their names. Right now… the temptation to rip them limb from limb was too great. Right now the rage that had been trapped within the sword…

No… it was not time to unleash that rage but how he wished that he knew where that rage had come from.

The houses would need to be rebuilt. The castle… even from a distance did not suit this star… did not suit him. The streets

"It would be better if Magnar or Prim could just created what I think the city should look like."

A New World

Zale laughed. "Too much red and black rock and nothing else?"

"Too much… It looks like the inside of the volcano and nothing else. Where are the trees and…."

"What do you remember of Osiris?"

Magmas turned and looked at his friend. True Zale had been an adult when he left this place. He had spent time of Lunisita. But he… and his brothers… they all had been children. Just a little better than youths. So what did he really remember? And what had been a fantasy? "The castle had cream colored floor tiles. And the lava pools were warm not …"

He paused. No the pools felt warm because they were use to being in them. Where as being in the castle of Fire was a rare treat. They didn't live there so it took days to get use to the lava pools.

"Bah. I will find someone to make this star look like home."

For a long moment Zale was quiet. His eyes looking at the houses that were little more than mud huts. "No one has dared change the looks of this star or any star in generations if any." He paused kicked the dirt, "You should ask Kaida what she thinks."

"You think…"

"That you can't come up with plans to make this star look and feel like home. To be a place while you're among the stars that you can relax to. I don't doubt you. But I know my sister. If you're going to decorate something in hopes she'll be happy…' The rest lingered in the air as magma bubbled and popped.

"Fine I'll ask my wife her opinion. Just think of it… she now has four castles to decorate."

Coughing Zale gasped out, "Four?"

"The castle of Fire , Castle of Water if I can get Magnar to catch the Meg-moks, The Castle of Wind so that the damn Dragon can roost. And the Castle here."

"And the castle of Earth? "

Shaking his head Magmas gave a grim smile. "No, that one is being returned to the ground from which it came. All traces will be forgotten."

Slowly Zale asked, "Prim asked for that?"

"Uncle Donny did. Why I'm not sure. But that man ask for damn little."

A New World

CHAPTER 43: GOVARD

The forge was not what he had thought it would be. Not when it was said the best in all of the armor of the stars were made here. No what he was looking at…

A few dusty work benches covered in webbing. The hearth barely burning. Water in the pails stale and rancid. Nothing here said that this place had been used recently. Nothing here told of any armor being forged to the hardened steel that the army had used.

BAH!

… the craftsmen back home on Prim's star had a better forge. Better everything. Then again…

His eyes scanned the area. A tickle of memory scratched at him. Those who guarded this star had been able to surround them. They had been able to get close enough to kill them and would have if Magmas hadn't been welding the king's sword.

Slightly his head tilted to the side in puzzlement. "So what am I missing?" he whispered to himself.

"What are you missing? Boy, you're not from this star so you are missing everything."

A New World

The voice was old. But , Fey didn't live past the age of being useful. Unless…

He turned slowly to the voice. The man was old and his cane was holding him up. But it was the battle ready light in those eyes that had him using caution. "I am a friend and brother to the rightful king."

The man took a step towards him. His hand waving with gusto. "The child who wields a sword. Bah."

Shit if this man didn't yield to Magmas things could get messy quick. He didn't say it but he thought it. Knew enough that Magmas was in no mood to be dealing with anyone right now. "Perhaps you could explain…"

Two more steps and the man pushed past him, "You look with your eyes. But you don't feel the air around you."

What in the name of Darke did that mean?

"You come from what star? And the truth. I don't want to hear the blasted blue one that destroyed half of the race."

For just a breath rage ran through him. If he wasn't a guest here he wouldn't hesitate to run his blade through this arrogant piece of filth. If he was on Prim's star he would gladly flay this fool with a few words. But today he was a guest. One that was tasked with only seeing the forge and creating something for the battles yet to come.

Violence bubbled inside of him earning to be let loose… yet he tempered his movements. As of this moment the old fool hadn't done anything to cause the rage to be let loose… and simply being here, he didn't have cause to see this man as a threat. An annoyance for sure but not a threat. Stiffly he let his fingers hover over the dusty workbench. Only it felt like his hand was resting on cold steel not thin air.

Puzzled, he looked at the man. "Invisibility. That's what makes those of Obsidian dangerous. You have the ability to cloak what you don't wish to be found."

"You are learning. But what star do you hail from?"

After a long tense moment Govard finally answered, " Arcadian."

"Ah, the star of creating mindless dribble and calling it technology.So many secrets lay hidden within the ruins of the city. I wonder if those born of the star will ever unearth the truth."

By the light this old fool was infuriating. " I don't have time for riddles ." He turned to go. After all Magmas could pull the answer from this fool or tell Zale to.

"I leave you with one last riddle boy. Only one born with the blood of the star can wield the secrets that it holds."

A New World

Govard spun towards him. That almost made sense. "Magmas has the blood lines of Obsidian." Not a question but confirmation.

The old man smiled. Slowly he came to Govard almost standing shoulder to shoulder. "Not just Obsidian. But that of the first."

Why was this fay telling him… why…

He reached out his hand to grab the man's shoulder. As His hand reached out to the man to touch the dark red cloak that had covered his shoulder whatever enchantment had been used the man turned to nothing more than sand and the forge of Obsidian showed itself.

In the winds a haunting whisper, "Blood of my blood."

He couldn't deal with the words yet. Remember them yes. But not ready to deal with them. No that was something he needed to talk to Flint about. But the rest...Slowly he turned to see the forge for the first time. Oh the iron workers would envy this silver anvil engraved with enchantments. The fires burning in the lava rock hearths.

Waters to cool the metals.

But it was the books. The rolled parchment that seemed out of place. At least until he glanced at it.

Blueprints for weapons and armor that had yet to be made. Spells and enchantments to be braided into the metals. What that meant Govard couldn't fathom … yet if what the spells said were true…

He wanted to dump this bag of trouble on Magmas' lap and just watch as the king tried to decide what to do with the information. Yet he might as well get all of the information first.

How much time had passed since he had broken the spell of the forge he couldn't guess but those who worked within the walls were returning. Their quick glances told of two things. They thought of him as not a threat. Nor did they care about what he was making.

His dark eyes narrowed as he watched them shift around the large area. Two large hearths he had discovered. Seven workbenches and six anvils three before each of the hearths. Of course he had to walk into more things then not in order to break the enchantments but still.

A New World

Distracted, Govard focused on those coming in… had been watching them so fiercely that he hadn't noticed the large dark fey coming up behind him. "If you're trying to make armor in this forge is best to enchant it. All that … whatever… you put in there won't be much help in a battle otherwise."

If he wasn't a trained warrior he would have jumped. Being trained by Lord Donivan and knowing the temperament of a truly dark fey… well arrogance was in his favor "It's called technology and the last I checked I'm not a witch."

Slowly the man slid around him looking at the strange wiring. "Arcadian, bah. What good was their advanced weapons when none had the knowledge to use them?"

Slowly Govard narrowed his eyes, "I haven't heard any reports from the war before the final battles. If you wouldn't mind sharing?"

"Names Marat."

Since he didn't offer his hand in a friendly gesture Govard crossed his arms, "Govard."

"You are friends with the new King."

Not so much a question but confirming something. And the way too many eyes were watching him now … one that may still end in bloodshed. With a single nod

Govard smiled, "Friend. Brother. General under his command. With Magmas I can never be too sure which side of his temperament I'll end on. I just pray it's not the side that sees me as a threat."

There a threat dipped in humor should be enough of a warning. Or so he hoped.

"Hmp. His namesake is a fool. I hope by all that is light that this king holds a brain in his head and not the false ambition of his sire."

He didn't know the new ruler of Pallas but what was spoken now. Words said this close to the last battle… those were reports that they would all need. "Explain." Just enough bite in the word to show interest, not enough to make it a command.

"Walk with me to the palace. I suspect the king would like to hear some of this himself."

An ally. Here on this star. Well maybe this wouldn't be as horrible as they had assumed.

There are only a few children running about the streets ones that had returned to their home at the being house on Prim's Star.   The parents, should the children have any, would be seeing what they could set to rights within their own homes thankful to be back within their domain. Yet they would do so cautiously for many knew the War had yet begun.

Marat walked at a ground eating speed. His muscles tight almost tighter than those in his chiseled jaw.   Whatever this man lived thru, whatever this fey knew…   it would take more than just the new King deal with it.   Perhaps even Magnar wouldn't know what to do with the information that this Fay had.

" So are you going to tell me anything before we reach the castle?"

" Those who were housed on Acadia were ill prepared for defending their home. They had sent most of their warriors in preparation for the final battle. Hoping against all odds that the war would not come to their star.   They took a gamble and all that remains is rubble and ruin.   All of the technology that they created now lies solely within your mind.   I pray that you forget it."

He had known his home had been destroyed.   He had assumed those who had been left behind on the star had enough knowledge to protect and defend long enough where the warriors held on Prim star to end the war.   If there were any more of his kinsmen house on the bright blue star he didn't know.   Possibly
Flint might. Karnak…   he couldn't say for sure.   The only one that has that answer was hiding away within the Under Kingdom.   Knowing if Magnar didn't have the temperaments deal with the queen on her terms then it was not time for her generals to Step in.

A New World

CHAPTER 44: NICCO

Dust and dry air. The scent of men who were cloaked. This is what he was welcomed to. Well not him exactly but Magmas. If he took offence to the lack of fan fair or not , Nicco didn't know. Didn't care. He had sent here by Primitiva. Sent here by the goddess herself. So it didn't matter what Magmas thought at least not until the general pulled the sword breaking the enchantment.

Shit.

He didn't say it but he thought it.

In mist form he couldn't roll his eyes. Couldn't do a great deal of things but the words of the goddess echoed within is mind. Keep an eye on the boys she had said. Keep them out of trouble.

Prim had known something. Seen something. Even if she didn't tell him, he would would carry on as though he knew all of her secrets.

The shadow that had cling to Govard had been his way to get here. Of course, in time he supposed that he could have found this blasted star city. In time he might have even made the trip under his own powers. Yet what would have been lost if he had?

A New World

Staying in a mist form he watched and listened. Watched as Magmas had sensed the cloaked army that had surrounded them. Listened to the banter between Zale and Magmas.

Oh until that moment he had been ready to destroy this army. Ready to defend the boy who Prim wanted protected. He hadn't. No, Magmas needed to control this star as he saw fit. Still it didn't mean that he wouldn't aid him when needed.

A silent plea to the darkness and he followed Govard. Magmas could and would destroy every fey left on this star. But Govard…

… now he was trouble. Had always been trouble. Woman flung themselves to catch his attention. Men hated him for everything they were not.

Oh not in looks but in brains. In the ability to build the most complex contraptions for a number of different uses. None were practical but they all worked.

He had stayed back lingering within the shadows. Stayed back to get a feel for this place. So many things hidden from sight. Cloaked or shielded from the eye. The spells so much older then anything the goddess had created. If he could trust the feel of them … then they were nearly as old as the star its self.

Slowly he hovered just a breath above the ground. Slowly a approached the shimmer of room. A vale of power preventing him from actually touching the door.

It didn't feel right. Didn't seem right.

Magmas would be fine for a short while longer. The army here wouldn't stand a chance is the general and his lieutenants let their temper slip. Tempers that had nothing to do with the powers and abilities they all had before meeting the goddess, but everything to do with what had happen after.

No whatever powers Prim had unlocked would be needed. But even she didn't understand the reason as to why.

A steady breath and letting the boys go off and explore by themselves; Nicco allowed for his true form to appear. His eyes never leaving the door that had caught his eye.

"I wouldn't open that boy."

The voice was old. Not a threat. Yet he would amuse himself for the moment. Slowly he turned and gave a slight nod to the elderly fey. One of respect given to any of the dead. "I did not realize that the dead still stalk grounds of their home stars."

The man looked taken back. Surprise masked quickly but not quickly enough for Nicco to see it. "You know what I am?"

Slowly Nicco approached. A bone chilling smile touching his lips. Adjusting the cuff on his black suit he gave the man enough time to seem to be considering his question. Then a twinkle of mischief lit his eyes. "You are an apparition. Somewhere on this star would remain your body. Chained …" he paused , "… connected perhaps is a better term… to this star. It leaves you to walk freely among the living appearing to those you chose."

The man narrowed his eyes, "You know much for not being from this star."

"The creator has blessed me to see more then needed. And to hold her secrets."

"So what the boy … the one tinkering in the forge … said…"

It seemed though the man was speaking to himself and didn't need nor want an answer.

"Magmas will rule this star. But Govard is mindless dribble most days."

The man turned, "It is not time for what is behind that door to be needed."

"Very well. I will yield to the first king of Obsidian."

"Y-you knew…"

Gently Nicco eased up beside the man his hand resting on his shoulder. "Very few would know the feel of a royal fey. Even less would understand the age of an apparition."

"And far less could touch one without permission."

With a wink Nicco smiled, "Another time I would like to see who could kill who. All in good fun of course. But I think the new king should meet the former."

"Bah. He is young and foolish. I can taste the uncertainty within him."

"He is young but raised by a creator. And your sword chose him. I think that means something."

The old fey took a breath, "I will see what the new king is before I decide."

A cold laugh slipped from Nicco's lips. "Make him work for your favor. He will appreciate it more."

A New World

Forgotten was the cloaked room. Forgotten was the way the whole city changed responding to Magmas' every desire. Magnar had arrived. His intentions…

Nicco narrowed his eyes still staying near a shadow. Magmas hadn't picked up on his being here… and Magnar had no reason to think the first king of the Eostre would be here. No reason at all.

But that begged to question why the creator was here and who was the boy that he had brought?

Following the anger… the rage that flowed off of Magnar was unmistakable . It would not end well once the creator reached Magmas and the others.

"Shit." Nicco cursed. This needed to stop before it could begin. And there was only one person Magnar would respond to without bloodshed.

Prim was going to kill him for disturbing her.

He hated to intrude on her. Hated seeing her wrapped around Shesha shedding tears creating a pool of crystal. He hated this.

A soft cough and Shesha moved his massive cloud white head. The hate in those dark eyes then slowly recognition. He nuzzled her once blowing warm air.. "My queen." His voice holding the grief that Prim was showing.

She sat back her long red hair clinging to her body. Wiping her eyes she turned. "I need to be alone Nicco."

Bowing his head slightly he whispered, "I wouldn't have came but…"

She sniffled once, "But… damn you I have lost everything and you stand there…"

"Magnar seeks to control Obsidian."

Slowly she got her her feet. Gasping for a few breaths to clear the tears from her voice she nodded. Her fiery red hair damp from sweat and tears stuck to her face.

A New World

"This one time I will settle this. Magnar is my equal but he does not see all that I do."

CHAPTER 45: GOVARD

Not one of them drew an easy breath until the goddess slipped back into the shadow from which she had came. Not one of them dared ask Nicco nor Magnar a single question until the room felt less feral.

Crossing his muscular arms Govard Finally found his voice. "So now that we have the Prim all good and pissed off, Who wants to discuss the boy?"

Magmas narrowed his eyes finally taking a seat upon his throne. Slowly he placed the sword at his side allowing it to rest next to his seat but no longer attached at his side. He was trying to convey that he didn't see the boy a threat. It might have worked if the First king of Obsidian hadn't appeared to his right.

"So you bring a succedaneum into my realm."

Govard narrowed his eyes. The apparition did not sound cranky nor old. No the man sounded no older than the rest of them. His eyes that had been nothing more than translucent dark orbs now blazed with fire.

Shit.

The apparition was pissed. The rage that was pouring off of him was equal to if not more intense than that of the

Goddess who had just left. And that rage was directed to the only other creator known to be alive today. And that rage was starting to be seen in the eyes of Magmas.

He needed to do something before Magmas or this apparition Did something one or both may regret once tempers eased back. Shifting from one foot to the other He let his gaze fall on the boy, "So what is a succedaneum?"

A growl filled the room low and dark. The fingers of the apparition slowly curled into fist… his fingers more of a dragon then of a man. "They are the scourge of the realm. Bottom feeders. Those who dwell in the skin of another."

Slowly Brazen stepped forward, "What you say is true. What my people are… you think of us as bottom feeders. Yet we need little for substance. We take form in others only out of necessity. Out of the need to thrive. Would you ask us to die just because we are different from you?"

Slowly Magmas leaned forward. The move seemed to be passive enough. Any that know him, knew that he could out of that chair and cross the room with a blade to the boy's throat before any could dare draw a breath… Yet he didn't move.

"I would like to know more about this living in the skin of another. It may offer a solution to a problem."

"Bah. This boy will bring nothing but distraction to this star. He should be killed here and now."

" Uzziah, You forget your place. You are no longer the ruler of this realm. And I would like to know more before we decide anything."

"Uzziah? None have called me that since…"

Raising but one eyebrow Magmas leaned back in his seat. His shoulders relaxing, "Your sword offers much. Now since Prim had no reaction to the boy… Please enlighten me."

Looking to back to Magnar , Brazen slowly approached the dais. "My race hails from Nexus. Most are considered the undead. Our touch poisonous to most. Unable to be killed in the truest sense of the word. Yet we hold very little power compared to the rest of the Fey."

"As an admiral in the dragon army, I've seen your race fight, There is no need to temper your words here."

Admiral? What had Prim promoted Magmas… No best not to ask. Not yet. Not when the boy and the king were reaching some kind of unspoken truce.

"Then what you seen were the once who had not yet clasped on to the whole of death. You fought beside the ones who who in some ways still held the mirror of life. My race is very complex. A darkness that few can survive. A need to destroy the veil of life that we come in contact with. Yet we still thrive in the rays of the light. Even the queen of Nexus has yet to uncover all that we are."

Sliding up closer to the boy, Govard placed his hand upon his shoulder. "As enlightening as this is. What does it have to do with anything?"

With his head tilted to the side and a quick motion, Brazen gasped the arm that held him. Two breaths and he mirrored Govard right down his armor. "This is what it means to be a succedaneum." His head tilted to the other way listing to something only he could hear. A moment more and Brazen stood back in his true form. "The goddess gave you a second life. Unlocked abilities and knowledge that had been lost. Your fate is tied to another war… another battle yet you stand before me here and now. I know all your secrets General Govard, and I now hold all of your abilities."

"You… "

Not Magmas, not those Prim has sent here but that gasp coming from Magnar. A gasp that he rarely used. A sound that few ever heard.

"... The queen of Nexus should have warned me."

Looking like nothing more than an innocent child Brazen smiled, "You came to her seeking help. Yet you never asked the question you should have. She is not a fey who is complacent in giving aid without knowing to whom she gives it to. "

A quick cough from Magmas to cover the fact he was trying not to laugh. "So, if you mirrored me…"

"I would hold your secrets. Your abilities as they are the moment we are one. But you should know, Should we be not in the same place you would know all that I see and hear. Given to you in a dream. Should something need corrected you should only need to explain the correction."

"And why should the King of Obsidian trust you? Why should Obsidian yield to you boy?"

Magmas shook his head, "Obsidian shall never yield to this boy. However, his talents will be useful. Govard, you and Zale… I want to know everything our young friend is able to tell us. But for now , Magnar needs to go back to Feyen. And Nicco…"

"I am to remain here for a short time longer."

"Ah , good then I task you with showing the boy around the city. I trust you well tell me if something needs my attention."

Nicco's sharp smile was not comforting but he nodded. "I'll promise not to make a snack out of your citizens … this time."

A New World

Keeping his voice low and noticing the apparition that had vanished once again, Govard licked his lips,"So what do you think?"

Magmas got up from his throne every move tempered. His eyes not yet willing to look at everyone. "I think if Prim would have seen the boy a threat she would have said something. But I doubt this was his idea."

Crossing his arms Govard took a deep breath. "I don't like looking at a mirror image of myself… however, the strength that I felt in those minutes is not something to be taken lightly."

Marat who had not spoken a word since Magnar had arrived finally stepped forward, "The first king may know something about the boy's race. Or at the least his ancestors. Don't dismiss one and embrace the other. There might be more to this then just trick of the eye."

A moment a silence filled the room as Zale nodded once, "Mag… I'll follow your lead on this, But you can't rule two places at once. This may be the answer you need."

"I will consider it. For now I would like to be alone."

Watching Marat leave, Govard gave his friend a look. One that translated into Zale staying to handle the King.

EPILOGUE

A New World

CHAPTER 46: KING

MAGMAS OF OBSIDIAN

Cronan. The star of the dead. Second one to Nexus. The castle built from the bones of their dead. Or at least that is what was said. In truth it was dark stone nearly as strong as that of Obsidian.

The warriors divided in two. Half of the star sided with Pallas the other with the Dragon army. No one could be sure who fought for who. No one could be sure if the enemy wasn't part of the command.

Magmas Looked at Govard. Both of their golden armor already covered in the blood of the dead. So many more would surly die this day. "This could be worse."

Looking at Magmas and back to the castle Govard snickered, "Yeah worse. We could have Griffith here."

"Griffith? Naw I was thinking Kaida could be here. And a few dragons. I almost those battles."

Two steps and the rubble shifted beneath his boot. A soft rumbling. "Mag… we are among friends here right? This is a peaceful mission…"

His eyes was already looking to the sky. A swarm of fey in attack formation. Fresh and rested. "The castle. Get to the castle…"

They were among friends so why were the fey here trying to keep them from the castle. The King of Cronan was going to give this star to the dragon army… So why….

"It's a Trap!" Magmas yelled his onyx sword pointing to the castle. "In there!"

Too many bodies. Too many fey.

The wall exploding sealing them off from the outside. Two breaths, That's all they had till the bodies that lined the halls begun to move.

A flutter near their boots. A heart beat then…

A gold sword arched through the night. Steel against steel.

"Griffith?"

"Damn it Magmas. You're old enough to know a trap before you fly into one." His sword slicing through another enemy.

"How are you here?"

" Govard needs… to be …elsewhere."   His breathes labored trying to fend off the fey that were advancing.

"Fine. Down that way. The inner sanctum."

Dark stairs. Grunts and moans from up top. A wall to their backs.

Fool idiot. He knew better than this. "Griffith, take a shadow and get Govard out of here."

"I'm not …"

"That's an order General. Prim want's him somewhere to get there."

Griffith placed his hand on Magmas' shoulder, "This is suicide."

A New World

"No. I'll be fine. Now go."

His head ached. His body raged with fever. Slowly his eyes opened. Blurred vision.

Chains bound to his body.

He didn't know what had happened after Griffith had vanished with Govard, Never knew how exactly he had been captured. But that couldn't matter.

His vision cleared just enough to see the king of Pallas. "Hello father."

Magmas leaned over, "You have a choice boy give me Obsidian or die in the Prison of Nexus."

As long as his sword was safe they couldn't kill him.. it was of little comfort. More so when knowing those who entered Nexus never returned. Still he said, "I would rather die then give up my throne."

A New World

Chapter 47: Govard

One minute they had been back to the wall the next in another room. Griffith was holding him trying to keep him away from the wall. "Let me go… Damn you…."

"Not now. We have to go."

He swung at the air trying to vent his frustrations. "Go where? Damn you look around we just passed through a solid wall. To where. Look around Griffith. We are in the heart of the castle. We are safe in here. But Magmas is out there." His gestured to the wall. Desperation etched on his face.

"I know. I have my orders. Prim or Magnar or hell I don't know who needs you not here. We have to go."

Rage and desperation bubbled over as he gave his friend… his brother… a hard shove. "Magnar sent us here. Why send us here…"

They both looked at the wall realizing who had set this trap. "We have to go. I will trust that Mag will be fine." He had to trust because if he wasn't so help him , for he would do his damnedest to destroy Magnar.

"We can't…"

"Govard. Listen to me. We don't have time. You are needed not here. I will come back for Mag. You have my word. I will come back."

He looked around the room. Nothing here would be useful. Nothing to save Magmas. Just a shadow waiting to take them someplace else. "I'll hold you to your word."

He had not been here since he were a young man. But he would know this star anywhere. Wiring still filled with electricity hung oddly from the war torn houses.

Bones of the dead laid scattered across the landscape. Sever still clinging to the weapons that should have saved them.

His voice chocked back the sudden tears. Tears would be unacceptable for any warrior. "How long since the great war?"

Griffith squeezed his eyes shut. "Not long enough." A steady breath before he pushed on. "Come on. Magnar said the castle."

"Castle? I swear if this is another trap…"

"If it is he failed to inform Nicco." He nodded toward the castle.

"You know out of all of the first, I trust Nicco the most."

"Yeah well out of the first. He is the one that distrust Magnar the most."

It was hard to argue with logic with Griffith was right. The scary thing was with not arguing was Griffith was right. Still it didn't make being here any easier.

Turning quickly Govard grabbed Griffith by his gold bracer then locked eyes with him, "Go back for Mag. I'll deal with this."

It wasn't easy for Griffith to take orders. Wasn't easy for him to not storm into a room and demand answers. Slowly he nodded. "If Kaida goes on one of her war paths I'm tell her you delayed me."

Words coward came to mind but it wouldn't be spoken. No Kaida would have both theirs hides should anything happen to Magmas. "Go I got this."

The room was filled with bundles of wiring. The machine he devised so many years ago with his father. The thing that they never had got working correctly to take fey from one city to another. Yet that is where he found Magnar and Nicco. Both pressing every button, pulling levers, and having no idea what they were even doing.

"What the bloody hell are you two trying to do?" Govard growled as he stormed over before they broke something. And With those two that *something* would be him.

Nicco looked up over the console he was pounding on. A sliver of bone gripped in this teeth. "Prim sent word. You are needed here and get this thing working. Go to wherever it send you and stay there."

He stopped his movements trying to process the information. Prim, the queen, his queen, sent word for him to have a mission.She had told Nicco.

So not a trap of any kind. That cleared that up real quick and in a hurry.

Magnar being here then was to help get the machine working. Or mostly working.

That much decided he rushed over and looked at the broken globe and the two smaller ones. "The clear globe and the two yellow need fixed. The power needs to be conducted there."

A grunt from Magnar who looked more annoyed then anything but the requested globes were fixed with little fan fair. "What else needs to get this contraption working?"

"Do we know where I should be going. It helps something to put in the coordinates."

Nicco pulled away from the counsel. In a breath was in mist form before being whole once again. ""Blue star. Mirrors home but not." He shook his head, "I'm sorry Prim … she's not clear only that this will take you." Tilting his head he slowly crept over to Govard.

The move made him cautious. A feeling by the way Magnar snapped to attention he must have shared. "Nicco?"

"Magnar can figure out what he needs we need to talk privately."

Two ways private chats with Nicco ended, bloody or dead. There wasn't a reason for Nicco to want him dead, and nothing he could think of that would need him needing a healer. Yet he used caution when he followed the eyes and ears of the queen out of the room. "Sir?"

"Prim said you will understand your orders once you arrive."

Ok, so just a chat then."What are my orders?"

"Blend in. Don't let anyone know you are fey. Don't let on anything you know. Use caution. Exstream caution. Where you are going has two reasons. One if you stay among the stars you will die and the child that is needed will never be born."

"And two?"

"You're underfoot."

The twinkle of mischief in Nicco's eyes. Underfoot his ass. "In that case lets get me to where I"m needed."

The bright light, swirling colors and an explosion is what he remembered from the ride. A faint memory of of Magnar's rage. A glimpse of an image where Nicco and Magnar were fighting. Then nothing except colors and air whooshing past his ears.

His audible thud when he hit the ground. Then nothing.

The world was still. Darkness surrounded him. The shapes of trees before him. A light coming from above him. Moonlight. Well at least there was that.

"Now where am I?"
And that was the question wasn't it? No, wings, no markings that told that he was fey. So did that mean they didn't have fey here?

"Well Govard it looks like you are in the think of it now."

A New World

EXCERPT

THE SILENT WARS

OF LITE AND

DARKE

A New World

PROLOGUE

Her long narrow finger tapped restlessly on the dark marble table in front of her. Another score of Fey… powerful fey had descended upon her star. Descended into her country of Darke in the early morning light. They were scared and exhausted. Their armor bloodied and tattered.

The bridge that has brought them here now gone forever.

In the predawn light, she listened to the plight of the Star Cities. The war that her father was trying to shield her from. The war that would one day come here… to her lands. A war that no more use today, then had when it had first begun.

She had to do something. But what? The great generals didn't want her to join this war. They wanted to shield her for as long as possible. Her father… Bah! Who cared what he wanted. His secrets to great to trust his judgment.

Now with the dawn and the fallen warriors taken to rest she was seated within the room where her council could gather. Her anger seething.

"What in the name of Darke what are they doing? Do they not see there is another way!" her voice rose with frustration. Her temper barely contained.

Ethan glanced over to her knowing he was the only one in the room. And the only one currently able to handle her. "My dear, we don't know how they rule on every Star City. Nor do we have time to learn all of the laws that we need before you choose what side… whose side you will take."

Her eyes narrowed into tiny slits. Ethan was her husband. In the few weeks since they had bonded he had begun to speak more openly with her. His attempts at giving advice still new. As were his abilities and raw power that coursed through him. Still, she was not going to let him tell her what couldn't be done. "First off Lord Ethan, I am not choosing any side but my own. If they think for one moment I won't destroy both sides of this stupid war, then they are in for a rude awakening. And secondly, Lilly has already read and reviewed every law, every scroll, and every myth the damn Star Cities live by."

Shit. He didn't say it. Wouldn't have dared to. Not when deadly mist seeped from her fingers and her black dragon wings now were edged with deadly fire. No Ethan would never say anything when her temper was ready to flare. But his eyes said it all. "What I mean is your father has requested that you stay out of this war until all of your abilities are mastered."

A deep sigh and she tried ever so hard not to scream at him. He was trying to be helpful. It wasn't his fault that he didn't know what to say to soothe her. It wasn't his fault that there was nothing that he could say that would ease her temper.

Sitting back in her velvet high back chair she sighed. "Perhaps letting those who came last night restore the city of Manicora would be a good start. And I'll contact my mentor and see if he would be willing to see if the warriors could be trained for what I know is to come."

Ethan looked at her leery of her sudden mood change. As an Empath, he would know she was still bristling. Being able to tap into some of her abilities, he would understand that she was holding something back. A single heartbeat more and he asked, "What have you seen?"

There was fear there in his voice. A quiver at knowing that she knew more than she would ever say.

The souls of dead swarmed her eyes as she fixed them on a point of her meeting room. She didn't see the candles blazing along the long stone walls. Didn't hear the gargoyles whimpering outside. Nor did she notice the gate of the dead forming, but a few feet from where she sat. Warriors already clamoring out of their own realm ready for whatever their chosen queen needed.

None of this she saw nor cared about. Her voice becoming deep and dark. "Pallas will fall. The star being destroyed. The lives of those who are housed they're being consumed by a threat long ago forgotten. Swarms of locus feeding on the living. Absorbing their power. Four creators holding them back so that I can neutralize the threat."

Ethan swallowed hard. "How much can be changed?"

"Pallas can be saved if the damn rulers of the Star Cities would allow me to be useful!" the last said not to him but rather to a shadow hovering near her feet. A shadow that wasn't her dear friend and protector. But one that was able to move people through space and time.

A single breath and a Fey warrior stepped from the gate of the dead. His golden armor still shining and pristine. The emblem of the golden dragon still housed at its center. For only a heartbeat, he glanced at Nisha. His eyes scanning the room of long-dead warriors. All battle-ready and awaiting orders. Carefully, he took a knee, his head bowed with respect. Softly he said, "My Queen?"

Ever so slowly Nisha raised from her seat, poisoned mist burning the stones at her feet. A few tense breaths and she crossed her arms. "Uncle Magmas I don't recall calling for you. Unless you are here to escort me to the Star Cities so we may end this damn war before more Fey are lost."

There was no good answer to this. None that he could think of and none that would allow him to peacefully return to his own Star City. Still, he was not one to back down. "You're not ready to face what is waiting…"

His words were cut off by a terrible rumbling. The crashing of stone. The room crumbling to the ground around them turning to molten lava. For the span of more than a few minutes, Magmas glanced around. The castle was gone. The city no longer existed. Oh, the citizens were standing about where their homes and shops once were. Many huddling together. But there was no longer a single structure for as far as the eye could see.

Then the ground shook. Dark shapes forming. Fire erupting from the creature that Nisha was creating. A great dragon. Not scales. Oh no, that would have been less terrifying at the moment. No, this one was made from rock and dirt. Magma filling in the tiny lines to make the appearance of scales with the rock.

Slowly he looked to his left. Skeletons of races that no longer existed now fully formed with their flesh. Creations that only Prim knew once again fully alive and ready to attack anything that this queen found as a threat.

Gasping for air, he looked at his queen and fought long and hard to breathe. Her eyes were razor-sharp and completely focused on him. He had never feared Prim. He had never worried about what she was capable of doing. Never even after she had lost Alec had he feared for his own life. But Nisha was not Prim. And the terrifying truth, her powers eclipsed even those of Magnar.

A New World

No this was a fey to be feared. A fey that was more than just a creator. Since she was well trained as a warrior. Trained in the abilities of a creator far more than any before her. And the woman was pissed. "I…"

"Tell me King Magmas, Why am I not ready to see this war that has already annoyed my people? Why am I not yet ready to deal with your father who is the current cause of this war? Tell me, for I am longing for an answer." Nisha turned sharply and strode back over to her seat which was the only remaining structure that had once been a part of the castle.

Waiting for Magmas to answer she crossed her legs and leaned back, a look of stone on her face.

"You are not ready for the truths that are needed to be revealed have not yet come to pass." Not the voice of Magmas but that of the Fallen Queen Primitiva.

A quick flick of her wrist and the castle rebuild around them. "What truths, grandmother? The truth that Pallas is corrupted by a stone that should have been destroyed? A stone that you call the seer stone?"

Prim glanced only briefly at Magmas."Child?"

Recreating the table and chairs Nisha gestured to the empty seats and nodded to her army to return to the Under Kingdom. They would be needed, but not yet.

Steepling her long, narrow fingers she began to speak, keeping her voice soft and low. "The seer stone was once part of a greater stone. A source of power and destruction housed in what is now the Tomb of the Silent Ones. When they were defeated… or imprisoned rather… the stone was crushed. It's pieces scattered into the void. You, Prim, found one small piece and chose to trust what it told you to be true and absolute. Magmas, the current ruler of Pallas, found another. Its power only as great as the holder. Azia… we have confirmed, but a few years ago held on to a sliver. However, its power was tainted. Showing what needed to be done to restore the stone no matter the cost. Lies and truth bleeding together to yield the result."

Folding her hands on the table Nisha leaned in, "We do not know how many pieces survived. Nor do I have the time to care. But I can bet one is on Pallas and it corrupting the power that is housed there."

Prim crossed her arms. "How do you know this?"

"Magnar is a wonderful source of information. He chooses to bind himself with me thinking he could add to my powers not understanding that I already eclipsed his. But it did grant me the ability to unlock all of the knowledge that he has kept to himself. The knowledge found in the scrolls that he once brought there."

Gaping for words Prim forced out, "Th-The scrolls were lost after the battle with Azia. Nothing remained."

"Very true. They were lost. I just recreated them."

Magmas waited until Prim stumbled out of the meeting hall with Nisha following close behind her. Then scrubbed his hands over his face. Through his fingers, he glanced at Ethan, who was sitting much too still. "You forever have my condolences."

Ethan tilted his head. "Nisha, the queen, is formidable. Ruthless when needed. And does not play by the rule of any other. Nisha, my wife… " A long, deep sigh and Ethan placed his head on the table. "… I don't know. The lines of this union blur. I never fear her even after today because I know she will never harm me. But… She's not Prim."

"Meaning?"

"If I understand things correctly, Prim wanted a world where she was looked up as a great protector. She wanted to laugh with her people and never be feared. Nisha… Nish wants people to fear her. She wants them to understand that she will destroy any threat to her people or her family."

For a long moment, Magmas didn't dare speak. Carefully going over to the high balcony, he pointed to the sky, "And the dragon that she just created?"

Slowly Ethan looked up at him and half whimpered and half laughed. "She sent it to the Star Cities. It can't be destroyed. Even if something takes it apart, then more will be created, just as big, and just as deadly. She made this one knowing she would have an army by the time you agree that it's time for her to see Pallas."

Magmas shuttered at the thought. He had fought beside some of the dragons that Prim had once created. He had heard their screams as they tore into battle and know what it would take to destroy one. For this young queen still in the infancy of her true reign to be able to master not only creating one… but creating one that could re-spawn itself at will.

Oh, she was preparing for war. But he knew with all that he held dear, that it wasn't Pallas that this queen was defending against.

A New World

Excerpt

A New World

Dusk approached the light given off from Pallas slowly turning away till the morning was nothing more than a memory. The volcano spewing yet another volley of magma into the void.

Would the balls of magma one day lead to the birth of new star? Or would it become a tool of destruction of someone's home?

None could really say.

What the seers knew was still too far off to tell for certain. War was coming. That much was known. The light of Pallas may not lead to the divine as it was meant to. Yet none could say for certain if the war would caused by Pallas or if Pallas would fall because of some other threat.

Still they would prepare for both possibilities. Knowing the day would come they would need to chose a side and pray they choose the one that would allow for them to live.

A New World

He sat proudly upon his throne of bones. His trusted guards …. Skeletons all … stood proud awaiting orders. Waiting for anything that they may need.

Oh if he so ordered they would all collapse to the floor. Any intruder would think they were long dead. Long forgotten by time. Only a few would know the truth….

Those who stilled held flesh were necromancers. Those who brought back life to the dead. Sometime those brought back were given flesh and blood others…

Ah well, none could kill those who were already dead. And they did make effective warriors.

Another deep breath. Slowly blew out. How did it take so long to remove a child from one's body? Surely there was a spell or something to speed this along.

His finger tapped restless on the skull that had been placed on the throne.

Tap.
Tap.tap.
Tap.tap.tap.

Each tap just a little quicker. Just a little louder.

He looked over his shoulder to see the light of Pallas dimming. Soon it would be full twilight. A twitch of a smile. It should be fitting for the birth of his child to be born in the darkness. It's mother from the the light of Pallas itself.

Just as the last rays of Pallas faded from site a maid rushed into room. Her apron barely tied. Her round face flushed from running. A bobbled curtsy.   "A girl."

A daughter. She would never rule Cronan but… "Ah, tell my queen she should name our daughter Pythia. We shall see if we can make a decent match for her.